Domenic's War

CURTIS PARKINSON

Domenic's War

A Story of the Battle of Monte Cassino

Tundra Books

Published in Canada by Tundra Books,
75 Sherbourne Street, Toronto, Ontario M5A 2P9

Published in the United States by Tundra Books of Northern New York,
P.O. Box 1030, Plattsburgh, New York 12901

Library of Congress Control Number: 2005927010

Library and Archives Canada Cataloguing in Publication

Parkinson, Curtis
Domenic's war : a story of the Battle of Monte Cassino / Curtis Parkinson.

ISBN 13:978-0-88776-751-7
ISBN 10:0-88776-751-6

1. Cassino, Battle of, Cassino, Italy, 1944 – Juvenile fiction. 2. World War,
1939-1945 – Campaigns – Italy – Cassino – Juvenile fiction. I. Title.

PS8581.A76234D64 2006   jC813'.54   C2005-902892-0

We acknowledge the financial support of the Government of Canada
through the Book Publishing Industry Development Program (BPIDP)
and that of the Government of Ontario through the Ontario Media
Development Corporation's Ontario Book Initiative.
We further acknowledge the support of the Canada Council for the Arts
and the Ontario Arts Council for our publishing program.

ONTARIO ARTS COUNCIL
CONSEIL DES ARTS DE L'ONTARIO

Typeset in Bembo

Printed and bound in Canada

This book is printed on acid-free paper that is 100% recycled,
ancient-forest friendly (40% post-consumer recycled).

1   2   3   4   5   6   11   10   09   08   07   06

Acknowledgments

My thanks to the many people who helped this story take shape:

Sandy Cellucci, whose patient recounting of his experiences as a boy in occupied Italy during World War II planted the seed. And his wife, Loretta, for her assistance.

The monks at Monte Cassino, in particular Abbot Bernardo D'Onorio and Don Germano, for giving me open access to their monastery and for their hospitality and assistance during my stay. And Abbot Peter Novecosky of St. Peter's Abbey, Muenster, Saskatchewan, for his help in arranging my visit to Monte Cassino.

Farley Mowat, for his kind permission to quote from his book on the Italian campaign, The Regiment.

Ivan Gunter – like Farley Mowat, a veteran of the Italian campaign – for answering my many questions about the battles.

The Canada Council for the Arts, for financial assistance.

Kathy Lowinger, Sue Tate, and the staff at Tundra Books, for their invaluable advice, encouragement, and editorial guidance.

And Peter Carver, Mason and Hannelore Kirkpatrick, Annabel Lyon and her group at Sage Hill, Anne Laurel Carter, and Diana Aspin, for their support.

"To dwell in the cliffs of the valleys, in caves of the earth, and in the rocks.... I am a brother to dragons, and a companion to owls."

Job, chapter 30, verses 6 & 29

"The help he gave demanded a calculated courage that few of us could find for ourselves in time of need, and that fewer still could find on behalf of another man – a stranger and one-time enemy. That farmer was possessed of a spirit such as few men could boast. Yet he typified the true heart of the Italian ..."

FARLEY MOWAT in his
World War II book, *The Regiment,*
describing the help an escaped
Canadian prisoner of war received
from an Italian farmer who risked
his life for him.

Author's Note

In those countries where World War II was fought, few escaped untouched. Young teens, not yet old enough to be in the armed forces, were caught in the conflict, their lives forever changed. For those living in occupied Italy, in 1943 and '44, it was a perilous time.

The historical events described in this book are factual.

The Soldier on the Hill *1*

On a nearby hill a movement among the trees caught the boy's eye, but he kept walking for fear of attracting attention.

The boy was thin, his arms and legs made thinner by a meager wartime diet. His dark eyes focused on an opening in the bushes ahead. Beside him, water from the winter rains gurgled along a shallow creek bed. Both he and the creek were heading for the same place.

A figure emerged on the hill.

A soldier! And what else? A dog! A jolt of fear shot through him; his heart pounded in his ears.

Run! No! Keep walking.

"Just a boy," his father had said. "Just a boy out playing, they'll think. That's why you, Domenic, are the only one who can do it."

The soldier on the hill stopped at a rocky outcropping, lifted his binoculars, and scanned the countryside. Beside him, the dog – a German shepherd – waited alertly, ears forward, tongue hanging out, panting.

The hair on the back of the boy's neck prickled as the soldier swung the binoculars toward him. Ahead, through the opening in the bushes, a path led to the old mill. But he dared not go there now. What should he do? He stopped and looked down at the creek, trying hard to contain his panic.

Just a boy playing. Just a boy playing. His father's words came back to him, and he placed the small pail he was carrying on the ground and slid down the bank. The icy water of the stream swirled around his worn boots, soaking through.

Choosing stones from the creek bottom, he began piling them methodically across the stream. He didn't have to look to know the binoculars were still on him. A makeshift dam began to take shape, holding back the water. If his feet weren't so cold, it would have been fun. He dared a glance toward the hill again.

The soldier was walking in his direction.

Don't look. Keep playing.

He removed some stones from the top of his small dam, making a spillway through which the water gushed, happy to be free. Climbing the bank, he found two sticks, walked upstream, and placed them side by side in the creek.

The sticks raced toward the spillway, the larger one in the lead, the smaller one not far behind. Their different sizes reminded him of the two people in the story his mother read to him from the Bible. *Come on, David,* he urged, momentarily diverted.

Now the two sticks were neck and neck. Then Goliath pulled ahead. *Come on, David!*

The soldier was close behind him. The boy could hear the dog panting.

At the last minute, the small stick overtook the large one and spilled over the dam first. "Hurrah!" he croaked.

"You, boy! Name?"

He swung around and looked up at the figure looming over him.

"Dom . . . Domenic . . . Domenic Luppino." The dog sniffed at his pant legs, a low growl deep in its throat.

He froze, not daring to move.

"Where you live, Domenic Luppino?" the soldier demanded in broken Italian.

Domenic pointed in the direction he had come. "The farm. Back there." His voice shook. It was the first time he'd been close to a German soldier. The forbidding helmet, the thick black boots, the hefty ammunition belt, the casually slung rifle made him seem like some terrifying alien.

The dog lost interest in the boy and turned his attention to the pail.

"Where going?"

"If they do stop you, answer their questions," his father had said. "Tell them you're going to your aunt's, if they ask. But never volunteer any information."

Domenic pointed ahead to where a village steeple was visible over a hill. "There. My aunt's."

"What this?" The soldier pushed the dog aside and lifted a porcelain bowl from the pail.

"*Minestra*. For my aunt. She's sick."

Taking off the towel covering the bowl, the soldier sniffed the soup. He lifted the bowl to his mouth and took a sip. "Good," he said. Then he winked at Domenic and grinned.

Domenic looked up in surprise.

"Lucky aunt. Lucky you. Mother good cook." He swallowed another mouthful. Then, slopping some into his cupped hand, he held it out to the dog. *"Für dich, Wilhelm."*

The dog licked his hand eagerly, and the soldier replaced the towel and gently set the bowl back in the pail. The helmeted face turned to Domenic. "Strangers come, boy?" He was not smiling now.

Domenic shook his head.

The soldier made a pistol of his hand, pointing his index finger at Domenic. "If lie. . . ."

Domenic knew what he meant. He'd heard shots ring out across the valley last week. He held the soldier's gaze.

"Family, how many?"

I have to tell. They might come and look. "Six."

"Big brothers?"

Domenic stared at the rifle. "One."

"In army?"

He shook his head.

The soldier snorted. "Italians! You have hens, pigs?"

"Hens all gone. Pigs, too."

"All?"

He could answer truthfully this time. "We ate the last one a long time ago."

"Mules?"

"Just one."

The soldier gave a tug to the dog's leash. *"Komm, Wilhelm."* He turned abruptly and headed back up the hill.

Domenic watched until they disappeared. Then he picked up the pail and, glancing back once more to be sure they were gone, quickly pushed aside the bushes and turned onto the path.

It was a relief to leave the open field. He was grateful for the sheltering branches covering the seldom-used path, though they scratched his arms and face. The trees and underbrush were so thick, no one would spot the old mill until they were upon it.

A Dangerous Job

2

"You must never tell anyone," Domenic's father had warned him. He never would. He'd heard what happened to the family at the end of the valley. A German soldier gave their son, young Angelo, treats and asked him questions. Munching the rare piece of chocolate, the little boy answered: Yes, there was a stranger who came out of the woods. He was a nice man. Yes, he was still in the barn.

Domenic had heard the shots ring out across the valley. He found out only later what those shots meant. The father and the eldest son, Paulo, had been placed against a wall and executed for assisting an escaped prisoner of war.

"Fascist murderers!" his father had muttered angrily.

Domenic had been making the trip to the mill every day for almost a month now. How much longer would he have to do it? Maybe the war would never end, just go on and on and on. Guns and soldiers and shells and bombs, were they just a part of life?

One thing he knew for certain: The war was coming closer. He could hear the rumble of distant artillery, and see the vapor trails of bombers high overhead. And, just yesterday, a truck, full of German soldiers, had careened along the road past their farm.

The Luppino family had been lucky so far; the war hadn't destroyed their home nor made craters in their fields, as it had for many others. But each month the front lines edged closer. And two airmen had shown up, needing help.

"They're British," his father had told him. "Their plane was shot down and they were taken prisoner by the Germans. They escaped, tried to get back to their base, but crossing the mountains in winter . . . ?" He raised his arms, palms up.

Domenic had listened gravely. He'd known something unusual was happening. The night before, lying in bed, he'd heard his mother and father talking in low tones in the next room. The murmur of their voices had gone on for a long time, as it did whenever there was some serious family matter to discuss.

The next morning, huddling in the kitchen by the fire – the only warm place in the house – Domenic's father had spoken to him in the same low, serious tones. It made him feel important.

"They were desperate," his father said, "half-starved, couldn't stop shivering. Saw me working in the field and asked for help. I brought them some food and some old clothes, then took them to the mill. Nobody goes there anymore; they'll be safe . . . for now."

There hadn't been many German soldiers in their valley then. The occasional patrol had appeared, looking for escaped prisoners of war, or taking precious food supplies the farmers had stored up for winter. But it was rumored that more were coming.

"No one must know about the men in the mill," his father had told him. *"No one."* He'd leaned his face close to Domenic's and looked into his eyes. "Not your friends. Not the neighbors. Not the people in the village. Not even your little sisters. Do you understand?"

Domenic nodded, his eyes wide. He was proud to be included in the secret.

"Fascist spies are everywhere. If one person finds out, he tells someone else, who tells someone else. Sooner or later a spy hears, and then. . . ."

"I won't tell anyone, Papa."

"Someone has to take food to them. It cannot be me or your brother. Anyone who sees us will wonder why we are leaving our work and going somewhere else every day. But a young boy. . . ." He shrugged. "They'll take no notice. They'll think, *He's only going to play,* or, *He's taking food to his aunt.*"

He tapped his son on his knobby knee. "Only you can do this and not attract attention. Only you."

"Yes, Papa." Domenic's chest swelled with pride. Now he was an important member of the family too, like his older brother, Guido.

⌘

Mama came into the kitchen. Domenic could see the worry lines on her face as she took down the iron cooking pot, and he heard her sigh as she chopped a skimpy handful of potatoes, beans, and tomatoes for the *minestra*. It was what they had every meal now – that, and a bit of bread.

Domenic hauled in water for her from the well, and wood from the woodpile. Then he bent to his latest chore, clearing mud from a ditch so the heavy winter rains would drain away from the front of the house.

When he came in at lunchtime, his young sisters, Angela and Pia, were playing in the kitchen. His mother signaled to him, placing her finger against her lips. He understood – the girls were too young to share the dangerous secret.

His father and his brother, Guido, came in from the fields. Guido, instead of ignoring him as usual, smiled and patted his arm. Of course, Domenic realized, Guido would have been told what he'd been asked to do.

The family sat down to lunch – a bowl of the watery *minestra* and one piece of bread each. Domenic was still hungry when he finished, but he knew that was all that could be spared. Mama ladled the remaining *minestra* over bread in a bowl, tied a towel over the bowl, and handed it wordlessly to Domenic. He put it in a small pail with a carrying handle and headed out.

The first time, he'd been shy with the foreign airmen. He hadn't known what to say, so he'd said nothing, just handed them the bowl and left.

Now that his trip to the mill had become a daily ritual, he felt more at ease with them. They encouraged him to teach them Italian. "How do you say 'Good morning'?" the short one, Harry, asked.

"Buon giorno," Domenic said, when he'd finally figured out what he'd been asked, and Harry laughed at himself as he stumbled over the Italian words.

Domenic would have liked to ride Dolce to the old mill. He used to ride her to school on the days Papa didn't need her to bring in bundles of hay from the fields or baskets of olives from the olive groves. But that was before the school had to close, when the teacher was conscripted by the army.

Dolce was good company, someone to talk to. It would be too risky to ride her to the old mill, however. If German soldiers spotted them, they would take her. Mules were invaluable for carrying equipment and supplies over the mountainous terrain. There were never enough mules for the army.

In the mornings, Domenic would let Dolce out of her shed and fill up her water trough. Then he'd brush her thick coat, explaining that there were no more sugar lumps for her because of the war, and the apples, too, were all gone, but maybe someday. . . . Dolce lived on grass and hay now, with a bit of oats as a special treat.

Her temperament, however, was still as sweet as ever. That's why he'd named her Dolce.

⌘

The front was edging closer, everyone knew. Six months before, the Allied armies had swarmed ashore in the south of Italy. Troops from many countries – Britain, America, Canada, India, New Zealand, France – had battled their way north, up the Italian boot, slowly driving back the German army. The Italian dictator, Mussolini, who had supported the Germans, fled. A caretaker government surrendered to the Allies, greeted as liberators by the Italian people.

The German army, however, refused to give up Italy. They still occupied the northern half of the country, and Hitler ordered his army commanders to hold the line south of Rome, at all costs.

Domenic and his family could hear the distant *whump* of bombs and the rumble of artillery. Small planes flew low along their valley, disappearing over the hills pursued by puffs of antiaircraft fire. Allied reconnaissance planes, someone said, looking for German troop movements. The American and British air forces ruled the skies.

Not the ground, though. The German army still ruled the ground. But an army must have food. As Napoleon said: An army marches on its stomach. Allied bombers, however, were playing havoc with their supply lines from the north, and the German army had to get food wherever they could find it. They took cows, sheep, pigs, and chickens; they took wheat, barley, potatoes, olives, and beans.

But farm families had to eat too. It became a battle of wits. Domenic and Guido helped their father fill clay pots with grains and vegetables from the fall harvest. Then they took the pots to the field at night and buried them. In the darkness, Domenic would watch the flashes of artillery lighting the sky to the south.

Their last pig was slaughtered before it could be taken. Domenic's mother cooked it, put the meat in pots, and poured hot fat over the meat to preserve it. When they had cooled, these pots, too, were buried in the fields.

More German soldiers came to the valley as a cold wet fall turned into a colder, wetter winter. Stories circulated of men being taken from their farms as slave labor – to build concrete underground bunkers and gun emplacements for the Germans. The lucky ones slipped away in time and went into hiding in the mountains and remote valleys.

Domenic's father and Guido knew there would come a time when they, too, would have to leave. "You will be the man of the house then," Papa said to Domenic.

Domenic nodded. It sounded important and he hoped he could do it. He flexed his skinny arms and wished he had muscles like his big brother.

With few, if any, sources of news, no one really knew why German soldiers were pouring into the Luppinos' valley. There were only rumors:

"The Allies are winning."

"But they say the Germans have a secret weapon."

"The Americans are at Monte Cassino. They will soon be here."

"No, they will never get past Monte Cassino. No army in history has ever captured Monte Cassino."

Domenic, of course, didn't know any more than anyone else what was actually happening to the south. He only knew that he would soon be the man of the house, and that more German soldiers were coming to their valley. And that the outcome, everyone agreed, depended on what happened at Monte Cassino.

He knew where it was — the mountain, some twenty kilometers to the south, on top of which stood the great monastery. *But why should it all depend on Monte Cassino?* he wondered.

In the Old Mill

3

*H*arry's pacing became more frantic. Back and forth, back and forth, from the pile of straw to the tiny window and back.

His pacing irritated Jerome. Why couldn't he calm down, find something else to do besides pace? Yet Jerome didn't say anything. It would be easy to get another quarrel going. Like their argument a few days ago about leaving the old mill. "Let's take our chances and head south," Harry had said. "Just keep going till we find our front line."

"Put a sock in it, Harry," Jerome had said. "We'd either be grabbed by the Jerries and put up against the wall, or get lost in the mountains again and freeze to death – like we almost did before Signore Luppino found us."

As a pilot officer, Jerome was, theoretically, in charge over the young corporal, if you came right down to it. But he knew it was ridiculous, in this situation, to say that anyone was in charge. He had to use persuasion.

"If we hold out a little longer, the army will reach us. They're already at Monte Cassino."

That had ended the argument – for the moment.

Jerome studied the piece of wood he was whittling. It was supposed to be the head of a woman, but he wasn't much of a whittler – her nose looked more like the spout of a kettle.

Still, it gave him something to do. Kept him from thinking too much – thinking about friends who hadn't returned from missions. And how close he'd come himself – like the last time, when antiaircraft flak had sent their bomber spiraling earthward, engines on fire, he and Harry getting out just in time. Drifting down, he'd searched the sky for more white blossoms, but there were none. He'd realized, with a sickening feeling, that the others had gone down with the plane.

If he did get back in action, how long before he, too, ran out of luck?

Still, it could be worse, he told himself. In the air force, a hot meal and a comfortable bed were waiting for a flyer when he returned from a mission – if he returned. Not for his brother in the infantry, though. He had to live where he fought, sleeping in a foxhole – if the ground wasn't too frozen to dig – eating cold bully beef and hard biscuits. The infantryman had it tough twenty-four hours a day.

Especially on Monte Cassino, where the Allied troops were fighting now. Mortar bombs raining down on them at night; German snipers waiting above all day – waiting for someone to raise his head, then *POW!* Rain, snow, steep slippery trails, mines, artillery shells, cold, wet, short of food, short of ammunition, short of sleep, short of everything. Short of life, many of them. Fight all night – attack and gain a crucial ridge, a German counterattack and they gain it back. Lie doggo all day and take your life in your hands to even go for a pee.

Jerome hoped his brother wasn't on Monte Cassino. Last time he'd seen him – when his brother had a few days' leave and came to the air base – they'd talked about it.

The generals, in their twelve-hundred-room castle in Naples, kept ordering more attacks, his brother told him – the British general, Sir Harold Alexander, and under him, the New Zealand general, Sir Bernard Freyberg, holder of a Victoria Cross and a man of unquestioned bravery, but impulsive in his decisions. The ambitious young American general, Mark Clark, too, though Clark chose to stay in a trailer on the grounds for PR reasons.

Convinced that just one more push would take Monte Cassino, the generals stubbornly ordered attack after attack from their castle headquarters. Each one bloody, each fruitless. An American lieutenant said he saw dead and wounded GI's all over the mountain, but he never saw a senior officer in all the time he'd been up there.

Jerome thought of the piece he'd read in an American newspaper someone left at the base. It made such an impression on him, he'd torn it out and kept it. Whenever he started feeling sorry for himself, he read it again. He took out the worn scrap of paper now.

By Ernie Pyle, an American war correspondent in Italy, it read:

> Our troops were living in almost inconceivable misery. . . . Thousands lay at night in the high mountains with the temperature below freezing and the thin snow sifting over them. They dug into the stones and slept in little chasms and behind rocks and in half-caves. They lived like men of prehistoric times, and a club would have become them more than a machine gun.

And they were expected to fight too, Jerome thought wryly. He tucked the clipping away and resumed his whittling as Harry wheeled past again, still pacing.

⌘

"Where is that damn kid?" Harry muttered.

This was too much for Jerome. He pointed with his knife. "Just watch it, Harry. Every time he comes here, that boy risks his life for us. You know what would happen if the Germans caught him." He glared.

Harry glared back, his fists clenched.

A long minute passed.

Then a bat squeaked somewhere in the rafters and Harry slowly unclenched his fists. "Blimey, you're right. I didn't mean that. But I get so bleeding hungry on one skimpy meal a day." He grinned and tapped his projecting ribs. "I'm a skinny bloke. I don't have any body fat like some of us do."

Jerome laughed, going along with the joke, though he had hardly any body fat left either after months on the run. He whittled another sliver of wood and his thoughts went back to the village where he'd grown up, and to his wife, Jean, and the baby he'd never seen. Only nineteen and already he had a family. That's what wartime did to you – made you want to get in all the living you could, while you still could.

He'd give anything to be back in the village now, but when he was younger all he could think about was getting out. Sure, it was nice in a way – one of his aunts was always good for a cup of hot chocolate after school, and one of his uncles liked to kick a soccer ball around – but then there were the others, always lecturing him on something, knowing everything he did.

Like the first time he got up his nerve to kiss a girl. She had red hair and green eyes and her name was Shirley. They were in her shed after school and he thought they were alone, but the next day the whole village knew, and Shirley's father yelled at him to stay away from his daughter. He still thought about that first kiss sometimes. How it had sent electricity running up and down his legs, and the astonishing softness of her lips.

Lying in the hay of the mill at night, listening to the rats scrabbling, ears cocked for a German patrol, they talked about things that Jerome would never tell a chap like Harry if they'd just met in a pub. "You were lucky in a way, Harry," he'd said one night, "growing up where nobody knew you, or cared what you did."

Harry hadn't agreed. "I think *you* were lucky. Mine was a bloody rough neighborhood. Coming home from school, you had to watch which streets you took. You kept to your own territory, or else you got a beating you wouldn't soon forget."

Harry had grown up in the slums of London during the Great Depression. There was just his mother, and later a sweetheart Harry hoped to marry someday. If she waited for him. If he ever got out of this war alive.

We both know everything about each other, Jerome thought. He'd learned Harry had lied about his age to get into the air force – they didn't investigate too closely in the desperate days after the fall of France and the retreat at Dunkirk. If you were fit and looked old enough, you could bluff your way in, even if you were as young and as short as Harry. In fact, being short was better for some jobs, like that of a tail gunner, who had to scrunch himself into the rear bubble of a bomber.

Now Harry moved to the rickety ladder that led from the loft to the lower level. "I'm going to wash up in the stream. Give me something to do besides think about food."

He was back in a few minutes, scrambling up the ladder. "Someone's coming."

⌘

The outside of the old mill's walls were overgrown with moss and vines, and its roof sagged. It was gradually sinking back into the landscape. Once, it had been a thriving business, the millstone busy grinding the wagonloads of grain brought by the valley farmers.

The mill had belonged to Domenic's grandfather then, but the business hadn't survived the Great Depression of the thirties. A swift-flowing stream still tumbled past, still eager to drive the mill wheel, and on the lower floor the millstone still sat stolidly on its supports, as if waiting to grind the next load of grain.

Built on a slope, a door on the upper side opened directly into the second-story loft. It was there that Domenic now approached.

The heavy wooden door groaned as he pushed it open. He whistled and stepped inside, conscious that two pairs of eyes would be fixed on him. Then he heard rustling and the men in tattered clothes emerged from a pile of hay. They grinned at him. *"Buon giorno, Domenic."*

He was amazed he'd been able to teach these important men something, even if it was only a few words of Italian. "Goot day," he said, trying out the English they had taught him. He yearned to talk to them more, to ask what it was like to fly an airplane high above the ground. And where they had come from. And how they got here. A thousand questions. Too few words.

He could only smile and lift the bowl of bread and soup from the pail – a bowl that was not as full as usual. *"Soldato,"* he said, pointing to the bowl. He racked his brain, then the English word came to him. "Soljer." He pantomimed the soldier drinking from the bowl, and hoped they wouldn't think it was he who'd taken it. "Soljer," he repeated.

The men looked at each other warily. "Where, Domenic? *Dove?*"

Domenic waved his hand to indicate that the soldier had gone away, and they smiled then and reached for the bowl. Even if it was only partially full, it was still the high-light of their day, their one and only meal. They sniffed, savoring the aroma, delaying the moment when that meal would be over.

The shorter one retrieved a similar bowl from its hiding place. It had been carefully washed in the stream to discourage the rats and German tracking dogs. Domenic put the clean bowl in his pail and turned to go. The taller one patted him on the back.

"Brave lad," he said.

Domenic wasn't sure what the English words meant, but the pat on the back from this important man who flew airplanes made him feel good.

That night in bed, he tried not to think about the German soldier. Or about the penalty, if he was caught. It was better not to. How much longer would he have to make the trip to the old mill? How much longer before a German patrol, or a spy from the town, found out why he was going there every day?

It took him a long time to get to sleep and, when he did, he dreamt about a fierce, slavering dog.

The Shelter

4

*A*ntonio couldn't help ducking as a shell whistled overhead. *The shells can't reach us here,* he kept telling himself, *not here under these thick walls. Besides, they're not even aiming at the monastery.* But it didn't do any good — gun-shy now, Antonio still ducked. The piercing whistle of the approaching shell reminded him of that other fatal shell — the one that had demolished his home.

He saw he wasn't the only one; others instinctively ducked too. And everyone in the shelter stopped whatever they were doing — stopped stirring thin soup over smoking fires, stopped comforting crying babies, stopped quarreling with neighbors over a few feet of space — stopped and turned their eyes upward. Even those staring vacantly redirected their gaze to the low stone ceiling overhead, as if they could see through it and follow the flight of the shell. A hush descended on the cavelike shelter.

Then the whistling faded and a muffled roar followed, as the shell hit somewhere on the far side of the monastery. The hush was broken by talk again, and everyone went back to what they had been doing.

Antonio had stumbled into this shelter the day before. "It's called the *conigliera*," he heard a distraught mother explain to her children, "because the monks kept rabbits in here before the war." A large cavelike opening under a corner of the monastery, the huge, solid structures overhead gave it protection. It was now jammed with a hundred desperate townspeople seeking a safe refuge. There was, however, no entrance to the monastery from the *conigliera*.

"We can pretend we're bunnies," the mother said. Shivering, hungry, and frightened, her children looked up at her blankly.

Antonio could hardly remember how he got here. He must have followed the others up the mountain from the town. The last he could recall was the sound of that other shell – the fatal one. After that, it was all a blur.

⌘

Early morning it had been, the family gathering in the kitchen, his father lighting a fire in the old cast-iron stove, his mother getting out what little flour they had left to make bread, his grandfather staring out the window at the flashes from the guns lighting the sky.

The thunder of artillery had begun well before dawn – the big guns, miles away, shelling the German positions on the mountain, and the German artillery replying. The town of Cassino, at the foot of Monte Cassino, was in the line of fire, and the firing was getting closer every day as the Allies pushed forward.

Signore Rossi, their neighbor, said British and American battalions of the Allied armies had crossed the Rapido River after heavy fighting. The Rapido was one of the last obstacles before reaching Monte Cassino, and the townspeople prayed for a swift Allied advance to save their town from destruction. But Signore Rossi said the Germans on Monte Cassino could hold out for a long time.

The town, too, would be bombed and shelled, he said, because of the German garrison there, and Signore Rossi always seemed to know. Antonio sometimes wondered if their neighbor wasn't a spy for one side or the other. Or was he just wiser in the ways of war, having been an officer in the First World War? For whatever reason, he was usually right.

That morning, Antonio's mother had handed him a pail to fetch water from the well in the garden. He'd been working the pump handle when the first shell landed a block away with a shattering roar.

"Antonio, hurry!" his mother called urgently from the door, and he'd bolted for the house. He was almost there when he remembered the pail of precious water and turned back. Grabbing the pail, he heard the whistle of another shell approaching, and ran for the house.

He came to, lying in the garden.

Dazed, he sat up. Something trickled down his cheek into his mouth, tasting salty. He wiped his hand across his face; it came away bloody. Shakily, he got to his feet, testing his legs. He started for the house again. Then he looked up.

There was no house. Just a pile of rubble and a cloud of dust.

Through the swirling dust, he made out the bottom half of the chimney, the only part of the house still standing. "Mama!" he cried. "Papa!" He clambered across the wreckage, choking, tearing at the rubble with his bare hands.

Soon he uncovered a twisted chunk of metal that had been a washtub. Under it, an arm stuck out. He threw the tub aside and gazed down in horror. The arm wasn't attached to anything. On one finger, a familiar gold ring caught the light. He sank to his knees and threw up.

The rest of the day passed in a fog. He vaguely remembered other explosions nearby, some men searching through the rubble of his house, a neighbor leading him away. Then he found himself in this shelter with the others.

⌘

"The town's in ruins," Signore Rossi told him the following morning. "We searched your house, but. . . ." He shook his head sadly. "I'm very sorry, Toni."

Antonio was still in a daze. Suddenly it seemed important to him to keep his name whole, like the dignified grandfather he was named after – Nonno Antonio, now buried under the rubble. They never shortened Nonno's name; he was always Antonio.

Signore Rossi put his hand on Antonio's shoulder. "Anything we can do, Toni, to help you. . . ."

Antonio was only half-listening. His mind was willing everything to be back the way it was – the family getting ready for the day. If only they could somehow start yesterday all over, like rewinding a movie and playing it with a different ending.

"It's Antonio," he said. He wasn't going to let his name be cut down too. It was the only thing he had left in the world.

Signore Rossi frowned and walked away. "But he's only fifteen," Signora Rossi said, when he told her about it, "and his whole family was wiped out. No wonder he's acting strange."

Now Antonio began to feel the pangs of hunger. Someone – was it Signora Rossi? – had handed him a bowl of soup yesterday. He hadn't eaten since, just lain propped against the stone wall of the shelter, thinking of his mother and father and his grandfather. And his cat, Thomasina, who slept across his legs at night.

He remembered letting Thomasina out when he first got up. Maybe she'd escaped. Skittish at the best of times, she would be far away by now, frightened by the explosions. Maybe she would find a barn and live on mice.

He stood up and went to the front of the shelter where Signora Rossi was fanning a smoky fire, trying to keep a flame alive. Other small wood fires burned nearby, for heating water, or cooking, or just keeping warm. The occasional gust of wind would send puffs of smoke from the damp wood billowing into the depths of the shelter, stirring up fits of coughing and loud complaints.

"I'm almost out of wood," Signora Rossi said.

"I'll get some for you," Antonio volunteered.

"Be careful."

He stayed close to the monastery wall, his eyes on the ground looking for sticks, branches, anything that would burn. The rocks underfoot were slippery from the freezing rain the night before.

The area near the wall had already been picked clean. Down the mountain a short distance away, he saw a shallow ravine, which looked more promising. Slipping and sliding across the rocks to reach it, he began collecting fallen branches.

Suddenly, the *rat-a-tat-tat* of a machine gun opened up to his left. He flopped to the ground, spilling his armful of wood. The gun chattered angrily again, then went quiet.

Antonio raised his head cautiously. He'd heard no *zing* of bullets. The machine gunner wouldn't waste bullets on him anyway, he realized; he must be firing at Allied soldiers down the mountain.

Then an answering thump came from below, followed by the shuddering crash of a mortar bomb nearby. He hugged the ground again.

The firing went on, the hoarse rasping of the machine gun above, the ominous thump of the mortar below, like a vicious quarrel between two irate players in a game.

He lay where he was and waited. When the mountain fell silent, he got up, quickly collected his scattered bundle of wood, and hurried back.

As he reentered the shelter, everyone was talking about the shooting. Children, frightened by the noise, were crying. "It's getting closer every day!" someone said.

"The bullets will be flying in here soon," another said shrilly. "The monastery itself is the only safe place left."

"But the monks won't open the gate," sighed the first. "They say they can't let any more in."

Signora Rossi listened, her mouth set, her arms folded across her chest. She had great respect for the Benedictine monks, especially the old abbot, but when her family was threatened, saving her family came first. "We'll see about that," she said.

The Barred Gate   5

That night the shooting outside the shelter grew more intense. The noise was constant. Explosion after explosion rocked the mountainside. Streams of tracer bullets flew, like deadly displays of fireworks. Bursts of machine-gun fire ricocheted off the monastery wall. Mortar bombs sprayed rocks, dirt, and deadly shrapnel.

The townspeople crowded to the very back of the shelter. Antonio, hemmed in on all sides by crying, praying, sleeping, snoring bodies, felt trapped. He lay staring at the stone ceiling. It seemed to be pressing in on him, moving closer inch by inch. He would be smothered, buried like his family. He broke into a sweat, even as he shivered with the cold; he could hardly breathe; his hands trembled. Suddenly, he couldn't stand it a minute longer. He jumped up.

Curses followed him as he stumbled over supine bodies to the entrance. There, he took in great gulps of fresh air while the din of gunfire and mortars played around him. *Better to risk stray bullets and flying debris,* he told himself, *than have the awful closed-in feeling of the packed shelter.* Here, at least he could breathe.

He stared up at the familiar wall of the monastery looming overhead – a wall as thick as an elephant's back – and thought about the time before the war when his class toured the monastery.

⌘

They'd been bused up the bumpy, winding road from town – back and forth, back and forth, from one hairpin turn to the next, the bus wheezing and rattling and complaining. Above them, the immense structures of the monastery, poised on the mountaintop, appeared to be watching their approach.

At the top, the bus rested – steaming and still panting – while the students piled out and were led up the path by a severe, black-robed monk. They gazed up in awe at the forbidding wall that seemed to stretch on and on. Passing an ancient entranceway, no longer used, the monk pointed out the one word inscribed in large letters on the brickwork above it. PAX – the Latin word for peace – the faded letters proclaimed, as they had for fourteen centuries, the monk told them, since St. Benedict had founded the monastery in 529 AD.

Now Antonio wondered if the word PAX was still visible over the old entrance, or had it had been obliterated by the exploding shells?

⌘

At dawn, the shooting quieted, except for sporadic outbreaks. In the dim morning light, Signore Rossi appeared beside Antonio at the entrance. "It will be calm for a while now," he said, staring into the misty rain. "The soldiers have to lie low during the day. They know they could be picked off by a sniper if they so much as raise their heads. But tonight the firing will start up again."

"For how much longer?" Antonio wondered aloud. Surely the Allies would soon win. So many Allied soldiers from so many countries, here in Italy – America, Britain, France, Canada, India, New Zealand, others too, so many he couldn't remember all the names – their armies joined together to drive the Germans out. And Italy itself, now on the side of the Allies. All these countries fighting against the one. Surely the German army would have to retreat soon.

"How much longer?" Signore Rossi gestured at the steep, mist-shrouded, rock-strewn mountainside. "Just look down there, Antonio. Over the centuries, many invading armies have tried to take this mountain. None has ever succeeded."

"Why, then, do they keep trying? It's only one mountain. Is it so important?"

"Indeed it is. Monte Cassino guards the entrance to the Liri Valley, and you know where the Liri Valley leads." Signore Rossi paused and looked at Antonio questioningly. "Don't you?"

Antonio hesitated; he didn't want to give the wrong answer. Why didn't Signore Rossi just tell him? He thought back to the map on his classroom wall. "To Rome," he ventured.

"Exactly," said Signore Rossi. "And the Germans will fight like tigers to hold the mountain, so their guns can keep the Allies from entering the valley down there." He pointed below, though all Antonio could see was mist.

"But the Americans . . . ," he began.

"Yes," Signore Rossi agreed, "the American army is very powerful. And right now the GI's are fighting their way up the mountain with great bravery. But they are not yet at the top. And there, just below us," he gestured, like a director explaining the action in a movie, "the Germans are waiting in caves, and over there," his arm swung in a semi-circle, "behind those ridges, waiting with their machine guns and mortars and grenades. I would not like to be an American GI fighting an enemy so solidly entrenched on a mountain. I wonder why their generals keep sending them up here to die."

He sighed. "No, Antonio, I'm afraid it won't be over soon."

Signora Rossi, who had joined them at the shelter entrance, reacted to this last comment. "Another night like last night and we'll all go mad. We have to get inside the monastery . . . somehow."

"But the gate is barred," Signore Rossi said.

His wife folded her ample arms aggressively. "Well, if you won't do anything about it, *I* will."

⌘

Later that morning, Signora Rossi gathered a group of the other women about her, and the next thing Antonio saw, they were marching resolutely out of the shelter. He followed, sensing that something important was about to happen.

They took the path along the wall to the sturdy wooden gate and beat on it with their fists. "Let us in!" they chorused. "Let us in!" The gate remained firmly shut.

The women kept beating and shouting. Finally, a small viewing port opened. All that could be seen through the port were two eyes, a nose, and a bearded mouth. "I have been told to keep the gate closed," the bearded mouth said, and the port was shut again.

"We'll all be killed out here!" a woman cried. "By the oath of Saint Benedict, you must show mercy."

Again the port opened. "We have taken in the sick, that is all the Germans will allow us to —"

Signora Rossi interrupted before the port could be shut again. "But the German guards are no longer here. If the gate is not opened immediately, we will burn it down." And turning to the others, she instructed them in a loud voice to bring firewood.

"Wait!" the bearded mouth called. "I will pass on your message."

⌘

The monk hurried across the courtyard, glancing nervously at the sky. It wasn't wise to leave the shelter of the buildings for too long. Just yesterday a shell had landed on the monastery, damaging the chapel roof and blowing out windows. He lifted the skirt of his cassock and broke into a trot.

Reaching the other side of the courtyard, he entered the building housing the monks' quarters. It was reassuring to be inside the solid stone structure. But there was no time to waste; he must deliver his message and return with the answer before the women carried out their threat.

His footsteps resounded down the long, empty corridors. Most of the monks had been evacuated to Rome, the Germans having urged them to leave before the battle began in earnest. The elderly abbot, however, insisted on staying despite the danger. He chose ten of the younger monks from among those who wished to remain with him.

Now the gatekeeper found the door he was looking for, knocked, and entered. Two monks were seated at a table. One, tall and thin, was writing in a ledger. He looked up.

"Sorry to trouble you, brother," the gatekeeper blurted, "but it is most urgent. I must speak to the abbot."

"The abbot is occupied," the tall monk said. "He cannot see anyone at the moment."

"But it is urgent, and only he can decide –"

The tall monk held up his hand to stop him. "The strain of the past week has been very hard on a man of his age. What is it that's so urgent?"

"A group of women at the gate – refugees from the town. They insist we let them in. They say –"

Again, the tall monk interrupted. "But where are we to put them? What are we to feed them? We can barely feed ourselves, and care for the sick. And the German commanders have ordered that no more civilians be allowed in."

The other monk at the table spoke up for the first time. "All that is so, still the Germans are no longer guarding the gate. We cannot turn the townspeople away, brother."

The tall monk shifted in his chair. "I am only trying to be practical."

The gatekeeper saw he was weakening and pressed his advantage. "The women say if we don't open the gate, they will set fire to it."

The tall monk sighed. He got up. "Very well, I will put it to the abbot. How many women are there?"

"About ten."

When he came back five minutes later, he sat down heavily. "The abbot agrees we cannot refuse. Let the women in. But only them, mind. No more."

⌘

Word of the threat to burn down the gate spread through the shelter, and through another small building outside the walls, also packed with refugees from the town. A large crowd gathered behind the waiting women. Rumors flew that the gate would be opened soon. As the crowd pressed closer, Antonio found himself caught in the middle.

Now the gate was cracked open by the gatekeeper. "Only the women," he began. The crowd surged forward.

Pressed from all sides by pushing, shoving bodies, Antonio struggled to stay upright. An elbow smashed his ear; his face was pressed into the sweaty shirt of the man in front of him. He tripped and felt himself sinking in a sea of legs. Then a hand reached down and yanked him upright. He recognized the big man who lived down the street in the town and knew his father. Used to know his father, he thought.

Carried along by the surging mob, he glimpsed the monk struggling vainly to close the gate, then he was through. The crowd spread out in the courtyard beyond, and he was freed from its grip.

He caught his breath and looked around. The courtyard was enclosed on three sides by solid stone buildings, four stories high, their deep-set windows attesting to the thickness of their sturdy walls. The fourth side adjoined a second courtyard, separated from the first by archways, and beyond it, a third courtyard.

The crowd thinned out, many disappearing into one or another of the monastery's buildings. Some, however, Antonio among them, preferred to remain outside in one of the courtyards.

"We should be safe enough out here," one man said. "They'd never dare bomb the monastery."

I hope he's right, Antonio thought.

The Intruder

6

For a week now, Domenic's daily trips to the mill had been uneventful. He hadn't encountered a German soldier since the one with the dog. Still, as he set out today, he was jumpy. He remembered the truck, with a dozen German soldiers in the back, that drove slowly by the farm yesterday. *What were they after?* he wondered.

He had watched it from the window. The truck stopped along the road, and an officer got out of the cab. He studied the valley through his field glasses, then said something to the soldiers in the back. When the truck started up again, the soldiers' guns were at the ready.

They're looking for something, Domenic thought. *Or someone.*

Then, in bed that night, he'd heard the sharp rap of gunfire. Staccato bursts from the far end of the valley –

where the truck had been headed. He waited, ears straining, for more. There was only silence.

Today, when he reached the opening in the bushes
leading to the mill, he paused and looked around cautiously. All clear, it appeared, yet he had a shivery feeling
he was being watched. *Just nerves,* he told himself. No
wonder, after seeing the soldiers and hearing the
shots. He slipped through the opening and started along
the path.

Usually he felt safer here, with the dense growth of
trees and shrubs on either side of the path. Not now —
they no longer seemed to provide the same welcome
shelter. Now each shrub was possible cover for a fascist
spy, each tree trunk a potential trap behind which a
German soldier waited.

Keep going, keep going, he had to tell himself. The path
seemed to have grown longer. He breathed a sigh of relief
when he finally glimpsed the old mill through the bushes.

The airmen, Harry and Jerome, welcomed him with
their usual grins, and the banter he only partly understood. Harry took the bowl of soup and bread from him
and, pretending to be a waiter, bowed and held it out to
Jerome with a flourish. "Lunch is served, your majesty."

Domenic watched this routine in amazement. It was
something a kid was more likely to do than a grown man,
especially one who fought battles in the sky. But then, he
thought, the one called Harry didn't look that old —

hardly any older than his brother, Guido, who would soon turn seventeen.

All three ducked in unison as a bat zipped by their heads, swooped upward, and disappeared among the rafters.

Jerome put down the stick he was whittling. He had a whole row of heads now, each one a little better than the last. He took the proffered bowl and sampled it. "*Umm, good*. Your turn, Harry." He held out the bowl, but his arm froze in midair as he suddenly took in the dim figure facing them from the far end of the loft.

"My God!" he said.

Domenic and Harry turned to look.

The man stood, legs akimbo, at the head of the ladder leading up from below. He was tall and rawboned, his blazing eyes and tightly clamped lips lending his face a fierce expression. His dark shirt and pants were patched and worn; the high, black, shiny boots, however, were obviously of the best army quality, as were the field glasses dangling from his neck and the gold watch on his wrist. He slowly raised a submachine gun from his side. A shiver rippled through Domenic, turning him cold as stone.

The intruder advanced toward them.

A fascist spy, Domenic thought. He stared in horror at the submachine gun.

"Who are you?" the man demanded gruffly, in Italian. "And what are you doing here?"

Not understanding, Jerome and Harry looked to Domenic.

He couldn't think, fear paralyzing his brain. What should he say? Should he try to bluff?

"Answer me!" the man demanded impatiently, waving his weapon. He spoke to the two men, ignoring the boy.

Quick, say something, Domenic told himself. He said the first thing that came into his head. "We're from the farm by the road."

The man turned to him. "And them? Why don't they speak for themselves?"

Domenic shrugged, helpless.

The man stared at the bowl Jerome still held out. He sniffed it and looked at the towel that had kept it warm. Then he picked up the stick that Jerome had been whittling.

"Not bad," he said. He looked at the row of identical sticks propped against a post, like a display in an art gallery. He nodded slowly. "I'm beginning to understand," he mused. "You must have been here a long time to whittle all those."

Suddenly he wheeled to face Jerome and spoke in a mixture of English and Italian. "You *Americano? Inglese? Canadese?*"

Jerome sighed. "*Inglese.* Now you know."

"Ha!" the man exclaimed. "Ha, ha, ha, ha." He laughed exultantly and lowered his gun. "I see old mill. Good place rest. Then hear talk. If German, kill. But what I find? *Inglese.* Ha, ha, ha ha. *Amici."* He stuck out his hand.

Jerome seized the hand and shook it vigorously, laughing along with him, the tension broken. They all laughed, even Domenic, as relief flooded through him. Obviously not a fascist spy, but who was this man? he wondered.

"This boy, he help you?" the man asked, gesturing toward Domenic.

They nodded.

"That good. All help each other."

Harry looked at Jerome. "Is he a partisan, then?" And, turning to the man, he asked, "Are you fighting the Germans?"

The man shrugged, speaking in Italian to Domenic, "My English isn't good. Do you understand what he's asking me?"

Domenic had a pretty good idea because he was wondering the same thing himself. "I think he wants to know if you are fighting the Germans."

The man was indignant at the question. "That's all we do! Day and night, we fight the Germans. Tell him that."

Domenic tried to explain that he didn't speak English, but the man kept talking as if Domenic could pass it all on. "I was in the Italian army, until Mussolini ordered us to fight with the Germans. Then I deserted. Many friends deserted, too. Now we fight *against* the Germans, not *for* them. Tell him that."

"But I can't . . . not much English."

The man stared at him for a moment, then shrugged. "Never mind, I'll think of something." He turned back to Harry, lifted his foot, and pointed at his shiny leather boot. "Officer boot," he said. "Last night, Germans soldiers. We am . . . am . . . how you say?"

"Ambush?" Jerome suggested.

"We ambush. Kill. I take boots . . . this too . . . and this." He lifted the field glasses around his neck, and held out his arm to show the gold watch. "Guns, bullets, we take all."

Domenic remembered the Germans in the truck the day before, and the shots he'd heard in the night. He thought of the officer he'd seen get out of the truck on the road by the farm. *Were these his boots and watch, and the field glasses he used to survey the valley?*

A long, low whistle sounded from outside. "That my friends," the man said. "I go now."

He went to the ladder and swung onto it. "Goodbye," he said. "Good hunting."

The two airmen and Domenic stared as his head disappeared down the ladder. The loft seemed suddenly empty. For a moment, no one said anything.

"Good Lord," Jerome said finally. "Gave me quite a start there."

"I thought it was over when I saw that gun," Harry said.

"Wouldn't want to be the German patrol that met up with those chaps," Jerome mused. "No mercy."

"They take no prisoners either, I'll bet," Harry added. "Never even heard the bloke coming. Kind of nice to know they're around, though."

Domenic thought it nice to know they were around too. When he started back along the path, the woods no longer seemed as threatening, the trees and dense shrubbery no longer likely hiding places for a German soldier or a fascist spy. *I may still be watched,* he thought, *but if I am, it's probably by friendly eyes.*

He'd have lots to tell when he got home. But on the way he saw another truck full of soldiers go by. He sighed. There were more German soldiers all the time, despite the partisans.

The Warning

7

*A*fter his ordeals in the *conigliera* and at the gate, Antonio was determined to stay outside, clear of the crowd. He breathed deeply, filling his lungs again and again with fresh air, as if he could drive out not only the stale air of closely packed bodies, but also the dust of his shattered home.

He found a corner away from the press of people, and from the sympathy of those townspeople who had known his parents. They meant to be kind, but he'd rather they left him alone.

Huge as it was, the monastery's many buildings, particularly the cellars, were now jammed. He would take his chances outside in the courtyard. The Allied shells, Antonio knew, were not deliberately aimed at the monastery, though several had hit it by chance.

47

Others stayed outside too, some bringing in bundles of wood and making fires in the courtyard. One man held a few shriveled potatoes over the flames on a stick, while the woman beside him heated a pot of soup.

At another fire a man sat warming his hands, his back against the base of a statue. When he saw Antonio watching, he gestured to him to come and warm himself.

Antonio gratefully soaked up the fire's heat. Surprisingly, the man was humming an operatic aria, occasionally bursting into song. Antonio recognized the aria as the same one his grandfather liked to sing. He couldn't remember the name of the aria or the opera, just that his grandfather had said it was a favorite of Enrico Caruso, the famous Italian tenor who died in 1921.

The man at the next fire frowned at the singer. "How can anyone sing at a time like this?" he said, morosely.

The singer flung out his arms expressively. "But why not, *amico?* We've survived this far, haven't we?"

The other man refused to be cheered. "Yes, but for how much longer?" He went back to staring moodily at the shriveled potatoes on his stick.

The woman beside him offered Antonio some soup from a battered iron pot. He sipped it gratefully. But when the rain began spitting down, he left the fires and took shelter under the covered walkway that ran alongside the courtyard.

It was called a cloister. Monks used to walk here, meditating, Antonio had learned when his class visited. A calm and peaceful place then, he'd been awed by the immensity of the monastery, and by the graceful archways and stone pillars of the cloister. Never could he have imagined that the cloister would become simply a place for him to shelter for the night. He lay behind a pillar, clutching himself for warmth, as the shadows lengthened and night came on.

⌘

The whine of a shell woke him. Where was he? In his room at home? Then he felt the hard tile under him and the marble of the pillar behind him and remembered.

The shell whistled past overhead, followed by the thunder of an explosion somewhere beyond the monastery walls. The nightly bombardment of German positions on the mountain had begun.

The cacophony of guns and shells went on. He could accept the noise, so long as he knew they weren't aiming at the monastery. His eyes began to close again, then sprang open, alerted by the scream of a shell that didn't fade away like the others.

The shell exploded in the courtyard with a shuddering crash. Something hit the pillar with a thud, and dirt drummed down on him like rain. Then everything went quiet.

Suddenly, a melancholy wail rent the night. He raised his head.

Again the wail, long and quavering, not far away. He got up and ventured cautiously into the courtyard.

Where the statue had been was now an ugly crater. Beside it, a man's body lay, arms and legs akimbo, like a rag doll that had been flung aside. A woman knelt by it, rocking back and forth, keening.

Antonio edged closer. The body was that of the man who had been cooking the potatoes over the fire, and the mourner was the woman who had given him the soup. The tips of his fingers brushed her shoulder. "Please, I'm very sorry," he said quietly.

He wasn't sure whether she heard him. In any case, his words seemed totally inadequate, and suddenly he understood how his neighbors felt when they tried to find words to console him. He turned away, leaving her to mourn.

For a moment, he considered joining the crowds in the cellars. *But no,* he told himself, *that one shell was a fluke. It had fallen short of its real target.* He would continue to take his chances outside. He went back to the cloister for what was left of the night.

⌘

With the dawn, the shelling ceased. The sun, which hadn't been seen for days, came out weakly, and townspeople began to appear from inside the buildings. Signora Rossi rushed over to him. "Where have you been, Antonio? I was afraid something had happened to you."

"I decided to stay out here. The fresh air . . . ," he explained lamely.

She stared at the shell crater and the man's body beside it. "You should come inside with us."

"Maybe tonight."

"My husband was able to buy a few eggs," she said. "I'll save one for you."

An egg! Suddenly that seemed the most desirable thing in the world.

Then his ears, sensitive now to any sign of danger, caught the renewed rumble of distant artillery. Was the dawn lull over already? He heard the unmistakable whine of an approaching shell.

"Come!" he urged Signora Rossi, grabbing her arm. "Hurry!"

Now everyone was rushing inside, all trying to get through the door at once. Antonio stepped back to let Signora Rossi in. The crowd pressed around him. Desperately he broke free and stumbled back into the courtyard. The whine grew louder, became a scream. He threw himself to the ground and braced for the explosion.

Seconds passed. Only a muffled detonation reached him, from somewhere close by. Another shell screamed in. Again he braced himself, but all he heard was the same muffled thud.

He looked up and caught flashes of white against the sky, like a great flock of white birds. He stared, puzzled, then suddenly realized what he was looking at.

Paper! Thousands of pieces of paper. They fluttered down and disappeared from sight beyond the wall.

He ran to the gate, pulled it open, and peered out. The blizzard of paper was being scattered by the wind, tumbling over and over down the mountainside. Some had caught on a nearby bush, like artificial snow on a Christmas tree.

He slipped out and ran to the bush. Snatching a few of the papers, he hurried back.

A group was waiting at the gate. "What is it? What is it?" He stared at the papers in his hand. "Leaflets. Some kind of message." He saw Signora Rossi and handed her one.

"It's in English," she said, then turned it over. "And Italian, too."

"Read it, read it," voices demanded.

She smoothed the paper. " 'Attention, Italian friends. Beware!' "

A hush descended.

"'We have until now been especially careful to avoid shelling the Monte Cassino monastery,'" she went on.

"Not careful enough," someone muttered.

"'The Germans have known how to benefit from this, and now the fighting has swept closer and closer to its sacred precincts. The time has come when we must aim our guns on the monastery itself.'"

A collective groan came from the crowd. Signora Rossi held up her hand for silence. "'We give you this warning so that you may save yourselves. We caution you urgently. Leave the monastery. Leave it at once. Respect this warning. It is for your benefit.'"

She slowly lowered the leaflet. "It's signed, 'The Fifth Army.'"

A hubbub of voices broke out:

"The Fifth Army? That's the Allies."

"Are they mad?"

"And they say they're our friends!"

"Mother of God, destroy the monastery!!"

"But why? There aren't any Germans here."

"Leave, they say. But where can we go?"

"Nowhere."

"God save us."

A few refused to believe the warning:

"They wouldn't dare."

"Destroy the famous Abbey of Monte Cassino! It's unthinkable. They're bluffing."

Signore Rossi had an unsettling thought. "The message says they will aim their guns at the monastery. But they know better than I that it takes more than a 25-pound artillery shell to penetrate these thick walls. If they are serious, they will bomb. Their planes carry 500-pound bombs, even 1,000-pound. I pray to God it never happens, but watch the sky."

The group drifted away disconsolately, arguing about what to do and shooting nervous glances at the sky. Many, taking no chances, hurried back into the buildings.

"Someone should take the leaflet to the monks," Signora Rossi said.

"I will," Antonio offered. "But where are they?"

"In there," she said, pointing to the building she had come from. "They moved yesterday to a place in the cellar."

He started across the courtyard.

"Give it to the abbot himself," she called. "Only the abbot. He will know what to do."

⌘

As he hurried through the doorway, Antonio nearly collided with a girl coming out. *"Scusi,"* he said. He stepped back, then stared.

"Aren't you . . . ?" *Oh, what* was *her name?* He knew it as well as his own. He'd seen her many times in town, when he was on his way to school and she on her way to the convent. He'd thought her the prettiest girl he'd ever seen and made it his business to find out her name. Now he had one of those mental blocks that sometimes strike when a person you know appears in an unexpected place.

He'd never had the courage to speak to her, but, as he was going to sleep, he'd sometimes dream about her. Now, here she was in front of him and he couldn't even think of her name. He looked down, embarrassed.

"It's you, Antonio!" she exclaimed. She lowered her voice. "I'm very sorry about your family. It was so terrible. I cried when I heard."

She knew who he was, even what had happened to him! He was used to seeing her in a neat convent tunic and shiny black shoes. Her tunic was now smudged and her shoes muddy, yet her jet-black eyes still sparkled, her long shiny hair was still neatly braided, and her bright smile still flashed, although only for an instant.

"Are you all right?" she said, as he stood staring mutely.

"Yes," he said, recovering himself.

He remembered hearing that she lived with her father and her grandmother. "And you? Are you well? Is your father here with you, and your grandmother?"

She shook her head. "Not my father. The Germans took him to work for them." Her eyes filled with sadness.

"I don't know where he is. Just my grandmother and I are here."

"I'm sorry about your father," he mumbled.

She saw the leaflet in his hand. "I heard about the warning. Could they really bomb the monastery?"

He glanced at the cross on the wall opposite. "They can do whatever they want, I guess. I'm trying to find the abbot. . . ."

"I know where he is. I'll show you."

On the steep stairway, looking down at her head bobbing below him, her name suddenly surfaced in his mind. *Adriana, that's it!* He just had to stop trying so hard.

At the bottom of the stairs, a narrow corridor disappeared into the darkness. They had to thread their way past the sprawled refugees, past the crates of manuscripts and the paintings lining the stone walls – works of art that had been stored there in hope of saving them from damage.

It was well known among the townspeople that the Germans had removed most of the treasured artworks months ago, allegedly to save them from destruction. Some said that a high-ranking German officer, with an appreciation for art, had transported them to the Vatican for safe-keeping. Others, more cynical, said the most valuable pieces had been sent to Field Marshal Hermann Göring in Berlin as a gift.

They reached a door blocking off the corridor. "The monks are in there," Adriana said.

Antonio knocked tentatively.

"I'd better go," she said. "My grandmother will wonder where I am. Good luck, Antonio."

"*Grazie* . . . Adriana." He was thankful he could call her by name now.

She smiled, as if she had guessed his dilemma all along. "By the way, do you know what day this is?"

He shook his head.

"It's Valentine's Day." She turned away quickly, but not quickly enough that he didn't catch a glimpse of the blush spreading up her cheeks.

He watched her walking gracefully away. *Valentine's Day!* He had talked to Adriana for the first time ever on Valentine's Day. That must be a sign.

⌘

"Yes, what is it?" a voice asked from behind the door.

"Please, I have an urgent message for the abbot."

The door opened a crack. "Give it to me then. I will see the abbot gets it."

Antonio hesitated. "But I was told I must give it directly to the abbot. It's important news about the monastery."

The door opened further and he felt himself being scrutinized by a tall monk. "The abbot is occupied." A hand reached out. "Let me see it."

Antonio stared at the extended hand. The black sleeve above it blended into the darkness of the corridor so that the hand appeared to be floating in midair.

He clutched the leaflet to his chest.

The monk sighed and opened the door. "Very well. I hope your message is as important as you say." He led him to a small room at the end of the corridor, knocked, and went in.

Antonio waited in the doorway as the monk spoke in a low voice to an elderly monk, on his knees praying before a shrine. His red cap contrasted with his pale lined face, but when he turned and looked at Antonio, the intensity of his gaze transformed the face, and Antonio saw only the piercing eyes as they examined him.

He motioned Antonio to enter. "Where do you come from, young man?"

"The town of Cassino, Your Grace." Was that how you addressed an abbot? If this was indeed the abbot.

"I came with the others, after our house was bombed," Antonio went on. "We stayed in the *conigliera* until the gate was opened yesterday." Was he talking too much?

The monk in the red cap nodded. "The Germans ordered us to keep all civilians out," he said. "But we realized we could no longer turn people away. I only wish we could do more for those who are here. But we have little of anything left to give."

The tall monk beside him cleared his throat.

The older monk shot him a look. "Yes, yes, I know. I must read the message he has brought us." He struggled to stand up, helped by the tall monk. "Give it to me then, young man."

Antonio hesitated. He had to make sure he was doing the right thing. "I've been told to give it to the abbot himself. May I ask ... that is ... are you ... ?"

The tall monk frowned, but the older monk smiled and said, "You are very conscientious, indeed. I assure you I am the abbot."

Antonio flushed. He handed over the leaflet.

The abbot took it and read the message silently. His shoulders slumped and he looked at it for a long time, then, wordlessly, handed it to the monk at his side. "You had better share this with the brothers," he said. "It is appalling news."

He turned to Antonio. "How was this message delivered?"

Antonio described hearing the shells and seeing the leaflets drifting down, and how he'd gone out and retrieved a few. "Then Signora Rossi told me to bring one to you. She said only you would know what to do."

"Dear Signora Rossi," the abbot said, "she has more faith in my powers than I do. Tell her I fear there is nothing I can do but pray to the Lord to spare our sacred monastery."

The Unthinkable

8

The warning sent the townspeople into the deepest cellars in the monastery. By nightfall, the courtyards were empty, the cellars jammed.

Antonio was one of the last to retreat inside. He took a final breath of fresh air, then stepped reluctantly through the door and felt his way down the shadowy, echoing stairway. *This must be what it's like descending into hell,* he thought, and the impression of hell was reinforced as he continued down. For the stairs and the corridors below were jammed with anxious people, wondering what new and terrible fate was in store for them.

As Antonio made his way through the press of bodies, the same hemmed-in feeling crept up on him. Torn between his fear of the bombs outside and the dreaded claustrophobia inside, he hesitated.

A familiar voice. It was Signora Rossi making her way toward him. She had her young nephew in tow, while her elderly father, helped by her husband, followed behind.

"Come with us, Antonio," she said firmly. "This way."

Numbly, he obeyed. But where was she going? Could there be any place more protected from bombs than the cellar of the sturdy building they were in – the very cellar the monks themselves had chosen to shelter in?

Signora Rossi strode resolutely on, up the stairs and into the first courtyard. Through it she entered a second larger courtyard, the others trailing obediently behind. They passed the marble statues of St. Benedict and his sister, St. Scholastica, then climbed the broad steps and on through heavy bronze doors into the great cathedral itself.

Their footsteps echoed on the marble floors of the empty, cavernous interior. The gold of the vaulted ceiling far above radiated through the gloom.

At the ivory altar under the immense dome, Signora Rossi made the sign of the cross, then led them past the graves of St. Benedict and St. Scholastica beside the altar to a narrow stairway leading below.

The stairs descended into darkness. At the bottom, as his eyes adjusted, Antonio made out a short corridor and, leading from it, three small but elaborately adorned chapels. He stared up at the frescoes on the vaulted ceilings, at the figures carved into the marble of the walls, at the bronze statues of saints set in the niches. No ordinary cellar this, more like an elegant underground church.

"It's the crypt," Signora Rossi said, a word which Anthony suspected had something to do with burial.

The Rossi family settled against a wall in the central room. "Now let the devil himself come with his bombs," Signora Rossi said. "Here, we will be safe."

Signore Rossi raised his eyebrows. "Safer than in the other building? This cellar is no deeper."

Signora Rossi nodded confidently. "But here, we are directly under the ashes of St. Benedict and St. Scholastica. Here, we will be protected." She seemed so sure, Antonio found himself almost convinced.

It wasn't long before others found out about the underground crypt and joined them. Feeling their way down the stairway, they stumbled into the crypt, perhaps drawn by the same conviction as Signora Rossi. Soon all three chapels were crowded with refugees.

Whatever the reason, Antonio's claustrophobia didn't return, despite the crush of people around him. Was it simply the high ceilings that gave him room to breathe? he wondered. Or something else entirely – something otherworldly, something to do with the graves of St. Benedict and St. Scholastica above them, as Signora Rossi claimed?

Beside him, Signore Rossi was deep in discussion with a friend. "Troops from India now?" Antonio heard him say. "Relieving the Americans on the mountain? No doubt the Americans are ready for relief. They must have suffered many casualties. . . . What! Only 106 GI's left from a battalion of 800, you say? And that's just one battalion!"

The two men fell silent, as though this horrendous slaughter said it all. Antonio tried to comprehend the bare bloodless numbers. He envisioned piles of soldiers' bodies on the mountainside below – perhaps, even, in the very ravine where he'd collected the firewood. Each body belonging to a family somewhere.

Still, there were so many rumors, he never knew what to believe. "How does your friend know?" he asked quietly.

Signore Rossi turned to him. "He has his sources," he said mysteriously, then lowered his voice. "Certain people have shortwave radios – well hidden from the Germans, of course. They pick up the BBC broadcasts."

BBC broadcasts? That didn't mean anything to Antonio, but he had a feeling he'd better not pry any further.

"My friend heard the stretcher bearers couldn't even get to the bodies, the enemy lines were so close," Signore Rossi went on. "The bodies lay there for days, until an unofficial truce was arranged. They just stopped shooting, and each side went out to collect their dead and wounded. Germans and Americans, who'd been trying to kill each other a few hours before, working side by side on the battlefield. Nobody consulted headquarters, they just did it," he said approvingly.

He turned back to his friend. "I wonder why the Allied generals keep sending them up the mountain to die. When I was in war college, years ago, Monte Cassino was the classic case of an impregnable defensive position."

Antonio felt a tap on his arm. Signora Rossi leaned over and whispered, "For you." She slipped something round into his hand. "We've had ours, this is yours."

As his fingers closed over the egg, he suddenly realized how ravenous he was. He thanked her, peeled it surreptitiously, and shut his eyes in rapture as he bit into it. It was hard not to gulp the whole thing down at once, but he forced himself to take his time and savor it. And, in the end, he kept half for Adriana.

Is she here? He stood up and looked around the room. In the dim light, all he could see were vague shapes. Then, over the murmur of the crowd, he heard a voice floating toward him from the far wall.

"Antonio."

He turned and saw her. She was sitting against the wall beside an elderly woman wearing a black head scarf. "I'm going over to help my friend," he said to Signora Rossi. "She and her grandmother are alone. Thank you for the egg."

Adriana made to get up as he approached. "No, no, stay there," he said, and he lowered himself to sit beside her. The old woman with the head scarf leaned out and stared past her at Antonio, frowning.

"Nonna, this is Antonio," Adriana said. "He lived near us in town." This elicited another suspicious glance from the grandmother.

"I used to see Adriana on her way to the convent," Antonio explained, "but we never spoke until I met her today." The grandmother's lined face relaxed somewhat.

He held out the half of the egg to Adriana. She looked at it in surprise. "Signora Rossi saved it for me," he said.

"But it's yours."

"No, I had some. Take it, please."

She hesitated, then took it gently. "If you're sure." She split it and handed one piece to her grandmother.

Despite the crowding, the entire crypt had grown silent. Tension stretched across it like an overtaut guitar string, the same questions on everyone's mind. Would the bombers come? When? Tonight? At dawn?

But sitting silently beside Adriana, their hands not quite touching, Antonio felt surprisingly calm. *Whatever is going to happen will happen,* he told himself. *We'll get through it as best we can.*

For the first time since the loss of his family, he felt like talking. Not about his family, though. That was still too painful. About school . . . how he liked chemistry, where he'd once scored a hundred percent in an exam, and about his problems with Latin, which he couldn't seem to concentrate on, and how he hated the boring string of dates they had to memorize for the history teacher.

Adriana, he found, was just the opposite. She liked history, with its human stories, and Latin, with its logic. They agreed on one thing only: A lot depended on the teacher.

Then Adriana told him about her mother, who had died suddenly when Adriana was just three. "Your mother has gone away," they told her, and she'd pictured her mother getting on a train like the one in her storybook. But why hadn't she said good-bye?

The night passed slowly. They slept on and off. Whenever Antonio woke, Adriana's presence soothed him.

⌘

He had no idea how much time had gone by when the faint light crept down the stairway, telling him it was morning. Beside him, Adriana was asleep, her face as still as the marble statue of St. Scholastica in the courtyard. He got up, careful not to disturb her. They would all be wakened soon enough if the bombers came.

He left the crypt and picked his way around the sleeping forms on the stairs. In the cathedral, a woman prayed silently in front of the altar. Otherwise it was empty, waiting quietly, it seemed, like everyone else.

Antonio gazed at the row of massive pillars, stretching along either side, that supported the vaulted ceiling of the great cathedral – pillars so large it would take three of him, arms outstretched, to reach around one. It was hard to imagine any force strong enough to topple those pillars.

Outside, the sky had lightened. The cloud cover was high and scattered. If the bombers did come today, they would have no trouble finding their target. He tried to tell himself that the warning message may have been a bluff, as some insisted – a trick to keep the Germans from occupying the monastery.

But he knew it was no bluff when he heard the first faint drone in the distance. His heart sank and he stood rooted to the spot, staring at the sky. Soon he spotted the silvery specks off to the west, reflecting the rising sun from their wings. The drone became louder, then a roar.

The sky was full of them, coming on high and fast.

"Antonio!"

He turned and saw Adriana at the bronze doors of the cathedral. She reached for his hand to pull him inside and they hurried below.

The Bombing

9

The people in the crypt waited, all eyes turned upward. The noise of the bombers reverberated through the chapels.

One of the more daring men, who had run up to see what was coming, arrived back breathless, eyes wide. "Huge American bombers with four engines." He had to shout to be heard. "Flying Fortresses, they're called." Families huddled together, holding each other tightly.

Like a thunderclap, the first bomb exploded. Seconds later, it was followed by another, then an unending stream of explosions that blended together into one long, continuous deafening blast that shook the building.

On and on the bombardment went. Antonio's head was spinning, his ears rang. *Can anything – even the great pillars of the cathedral above – stand up to this? We'll be buried alive,* he thought, like his family. He reached out for Adriana, but she was hugging her grandmother, her eyes closed, her shoulders hunched as if to ward off a blow.

How much more of this could they take? His instincts cried out to run. Run anywhere. Anywhere away from this unbearable onslaught.

Yet he knew the underground crypt was their only hope. It might collapse around them at any moment, but to leave its shelter would be worse. Crossing the open courtyard, exposed to the full fury of the bomb blasts, would be suicide. He remained, slumped against the wall.

After what seemed like hours of bedlam, an eerie silence fell suddenly, broken occasionally by the crash of a teetering wall somewhere above. Antonio slowly raised his head and surveyed his surroundings. Miraculously, the crypt was still intact.

Was it over? Or was this merely a lull? He stood up and touched Adriana on the shoulder. "I'm going to see what's happening."

He made his way through the debris at the top of the stairs. Emerging, he was shocked to find the cathedral's thick walls and pillars collapsed into piles of broken stone and crushed marble. The crypt below, he realized, had remained intact only because those walls and pillars had absorbed the mighty blows.

He climbed over the rubble, past the remains of what had been rows of carved walnut choir stalls, where monks had voiced their Gregorian chants for centuries.

A picture flashed into his mind of the delicate figures carved into the walnut of the stalls, figures so dark and polished and gleaming, he hadn't been able to resist running his fingers lightly over them as he'd listened to the monk talking to the visiting students. "Those intricately carved figures are called caryatids and putti," the monk had told them. "Caryatids if women, putti if infants."

Now caryatids, putti, choir stalls, and all were mere dust.

Antonio shook himself and kept going, past the scattered fragments of the heavy bronze doors. Outside, he caught his breath at the horrendous sight. For all that remained of the once great monastery were mounds of debris, with, here and there, the remnants of a wall still upright, or a huge block of stone projecting at an odd angle.

Dazed survivors were emerging cautiously from the cellars. Antonio was surprised to see the old abbot himself. Supported by the tall monk, he was looking around vacantly, as if he couldn't yet comprehend what his eyes told him: Everything he lived for lay in ruins.

"The cistern, too, has caved in," Antonio heard the tall monk say. "There is no more water."

A group, who had tried to flee before the bombing, surrounded the abbot. "We started down the mountain," one of them said, "but we ran into German soldiers and they made us turn back. They said the Allies would never bomb the monastery."

"We will all have to leave now," the abbot said, sadly.

Antonio was the first to hear the drone of what turned out to be the next wave of bombers. Again, he saw the ominous silvery specks approaching – much lower than the first wave had been. Then everyone realized at the same time that it was not the end, only a pause, and they scrambled for the cellars.

Antonio hurried back down the stairs and rejoined Adriana. This time he boldly seized her hand and held it tightly as bombs again rained down. *They've already destroyed the monastery,* he thought bitterly. *What more do they want?*

The second bombing was shorter, but fiercer than the first, the American two-engine B-26 bombers coming in lower with fewer but larger bombs. Relentless explosions punctuated the throb of engines above. Then the cacophony suddenly ceased and silence fell once more.

He waited. *Just another pause? Or the real end this time?* Surely the bombers had done all the damage they could, for no purpose at all that he could see. *Did they really believe there were German soldiers in the monastery?*

Though the first pause had proved to be just that, human nature can be indomitable. Once again, the survivors began making their way out, in the hope that it was truly over.

Antonio and Adriana helped her grandmother struggle through the debris on the stairway. In the cathedral they saw that the altar alone had survived, with the graves of St. Benedict and St. Scholastica beside it. Projecting from the steps of the altar, where it had landed, was an antiaircraft shell that had failed to explode.

"A miracle." Adriana's grandmother crossed herself.

⌘

Outside, the devastation was now complete. In the space of a few hours, the bombers had destroyed fourteen centuries of skilled labor and dedicated workmanship.

In the central courtyard, only one thing was left standing – the marble statue of St. Benedict. Though still upright, it was, however, not unharmed. For nearby, the statue's bearded head lay where it had landed, on a concrete slab, like the head of John the Baptist on its tray.

Stunned survivors searched for missing family. Monks bent over the injured. A woman with both feet gone lay in the rubble, crying for help. Two monks carried her to the gate. Antonio and Adriana went to the aid of a man tearing frantically at the wreckage. Together, they lifted a stone slab, but it was too late for the body underneath. The man bowed his head.

A slight movement under the debris caught their attention. They uncovered a child, smeared with grime but very much alive. The man picked the child up gently and held her, crooning softly.

Other survivors had managed to clear a path to the main gate. Antonio watched them leaving. "But where is there to go?" he wondered aloud.

"Nonna says we must go to her cousin's farm," Adriana said. "It's somewhere north of here . . . a long way. Come with us, Antonio. We'll need your help."

Nearby, Signora Rossi was talking to the tall monk, who listened patiently. She appeared to be in great distress. "Oh, Antonio," she cried, when she saw him. "They have taken Signore Rossi."

"What! Who has?"

"The Germans. Just now. They came here and took him away with others. They must work for the defense of their country, they said. To build bunkers . . . heavy work . . . and he has a bad heart." Her usually forceful voice sank to a whisper. "It will kill him."

"But that's terrible," Antonio said. "I'm so sorry."

"Where will you go, Signora Rossi?" the monk asked. She looked bewildered. "Go?"

"We cannot remain here," he said gently. "No one can." He gestured at the devastation around them. "Even if we wanted to. A German officer told the abbot they will use the rubble for building defenses." He looked about forlornly. "There will be battles fought in this place of peace. We must all leave."

Signora Rossi stared at the ground. "But there is nowhere for us to go."

Antonio looked at Adriana. She understood the question in his eyes. "Then come with us, Signora Rossi," she said.

"Yes, we will help each other," Antonio said, and he told her about their plan to find the farm of Adriana's relatives. He thought of how much Signora Rossi had helped him and was glad of the chance to repay her kindness.

She looked up. *"Grazie,"* she said simply. "We will gladly come with you. But we should leave quickly, Antonio. The soldiers might come anytime, and if they do they will take you too."

It was, however, growing dark by then and they would have to wait until morning to tackle the path down the mountain. Meanwhile, they went back to the safety of the crypt.

Caught

10

*I*t was barely light when Antonio, Adriana, and their little group gathered by the gate, shivering in the raw early-morning air.

The monks had already filed out and were waiting on the path for the German officer who would escort them through the lines to safety. When he arrived, the abbot, carrying a heavy wooden cross and with the tall monk at his side to steady him, started along the path that wound down the south side of the mountain to the Liri Valley below. He recited a prayer as he went; the rest of the monks followed and a straggle of refugees fell in behind. Once the difficult trip to the bottom of the mountain was accomplished, the monks would be taken by German transport to Rome and the Vatican.

There, the abbot would learn, for the first time, of the worldwide controversy over the bombing of his monastery – a controversy that had erupted while the monks and refugees huddled in isolation in the cellars. He would listen painfully to the account of how many, including General Freyberg, had claimed that German observers in the monastery were directing the artillery – a claim the abbot himself knew to be untrue.

He would hear how the general had insisted on the bombing before his Indian and New Zealand troops launched their ground assault; how his superior, General Alexander, dithered, but finally gave in and passed the request on to the American air force; and he would hear, to his dismay, that the resulting air attack was the heaviest bombing ever carried out against a single target.

Perhaps the abbot would even learn that the 144 Flying Fortresses, whose bombs destroyed his venerable monastery, were led by bomber number 666.

Now, as the procession set out, the last monk in the line – a spare, elderly fellow – turned and gazed sadly back at the ruins of the monastery in which he had vowed to live out the rest of his days.

"The monks are being taken to Rome, I hear," Signora Rossi said, as she watched them leave.

"But Rome will be the next battleground, won't it?" Antonio said.

"Not the Vatican – it's a neutral zone. They'll be safe there."

As the procession was about to move down an incline, the elderly monk at the end suddenly stepped out of line. He turned and started back up the path. When he reached the monastery gate, he continued on without a backward glance.

The procession carried on without him.

Antonio watched the old monk disappear behind a ragged, jutting wall, all that remained of the monks' former quarters. Evidently he was intent on keeping his vow never to leave the monastery. Antonio couldn't help admiring his courage; but could anyone survive alone in the ruins, he wondered, with no water supply and a battle going on all around him?

⌘

Now it was time for their small group to set out. They were heading in a different direction than the monks – not to the Liri Valley and Rome, but to the country to the northeast. They took a path that wound past German artillery posts down the back of Monte Cassino.

Antonio volunteered to lead. He had once gone with his father on a trip to the northeast. That was before the war came to Italy and he only vaguely remembered the dirt road through the mountains, narrow and winding, up which their old truck had labored. He knew it wouldn't be easy to find the farm where Adriana's relatives lived. Not even her grandmother had actually been there. But they had to try.

"It's my cousin's farm," Adriana's grandmother had said. "If we can get there, they'll look after us."

Now they picked their way down the mountain on the first leg of their journey. Behind Antonio came Signora Rossi, leading her young nephew by the hand; then her father, bent but still nimble; then Adriana, helping her grandmother. Half a dozen other women, children, and elderly men, who had asked to go with them to escape the battle zone, were strung along behind.

The trail was steep, rugged, and punctured by shell holes, which had to be detoured around. At the top of an incline, Antonio paused to look back and saw, for the last time, the craggy remains of the monastery. In the early-morning light, it lay like some huge dying creature, legs jutting into the air.

The path leveled out. Then, rounding a corner, he came face-to-face with German soldiers manning an artillery battery. He stopped in his tracks.

"Antonio, get behind me," he heard Signora Rossi hiss. "Quickly."

Two soldiers, leaning nonchalantly against a camou-flaged gun, watched them. The soldiers straightened up as a sergeant appeared and stood, hands on hips, staring at the line of refugees. Though Antonio tried to make himself inconspicuous, it seemed to him the sergeant was looking straight at him.

"Over here," Adriana whispered. He inched to the far side of their little column.

The sergeant beckoned to Signora Rossi, now in the lead. She went over to him, and Antonio watched her pointing down the mountain and gesturing.

"He wants us out of their way quickly," she said, when she came back. "The guns will be firing."

They began moving again. Antonio kept his eyes on the ground as they straggled past, trying to avoid the steely gaze of the sergeant. Only a short way to go and he would be in the clear.

Then a barked command. *"Halten Sie."*

They dribbled to a stop. No one moved. The sergeant said something in German and, the next thing Antonio knew, the two soldiers took hold of his arms. He heard Adriana gasp as he was marched over to the sergeant.

As if examining cattle, the sergeant looked him up and down, then jerked his head in the direction of a crude stone shelter nearby.

"But they need me," Antonio implored. "The old people need me to help them." That was as far as he got before the soldiers dragged him away. He caught a glimpse of Adriana and Signora Rossi rushing to confront the sergeant.

He was taken to the stone shelter and pushed inside the low entranceway. With no room to stand, he crouched down, dazed by the suddenness with which his world had fallen apart. He wiped his dry lips with the back of a shaking hand.

Caught, he thought. *Caught like Signore Rossi.* He, too, would be forced to work for the German army. If he was to escape, he must do it now, while the sergeant was distracted. He peered through a crack between two of the stones. All he could see were the legs and boots of a soldier standing guard at the entrance.

Then two other legs appeared beside the soldier's. He recognized the shoes as Adriana's. Were they taking her as well? Anger welled up in him.

She ducked and squeezed inside. "They've given me only a minute," she said, breathlessly. "We pleaded with the sergeant, but it was no use. 'Army need muleteers' was all he kept saying."

"But you, Adriana, are they taking you too?"

She shook her head. There were tears in her eyes. "They are letting the rest of us go."

He felt a surge of relief. She, at least, would get away. His hand, no longer shaking, grasped hers firmly. "Go then . . . while you can. I'll be all right. I'll find you again, I promise."

The soldier peered in and gestured peremptorily to Adriana.

She squeezed his hand. "Antonio, whatever happens, always remember that I . . . I. . . ." Her voice broke, and then she was gone.

What was she about to say? he wondered. Was it what he dared hope?

A few minutes later, he heard a shouted command, and, with an ear-splitting roar, the first gun fired and a shell took off over his head with a great ripping sound, like silk tearing. Other guns joined in. Antonio pressed his hands over his ears and felt the ground vibrate under him.

He thought of what was in store for him – leading mules up the mountainside while the Allied artillery did their best to blow them to smithereens. No wonder the Germans needed muleteers. They must lose them regularly to shells, or to missteps in the dark on the steep, slippery mountain paths.

So that was to be his fate – unless he could find some way to escape.

War Comes to the Farm   *11*

"Some people coming along the road," Domenic called down to his father. He was climbing the oak tree at the back of the house when he saw them.

Below, at the well, his father was fixing the old cast-iron pump. He looked up. "Who are they?"

"I don't know. A group of them."

His father put down his tools and walked around to the front of the house to look.

Domenic climbed down and followed.

They were a ragtag bunch, shuffling along in silence. Women, children, and old men. One of the women was using a stick as a makeshift crutch. A young boy had a bloody rag tied around his shoulder. A teenage girl's head was bandaged. She was helping an elderly woman to keep up. An old man carried a small child on his back.

Gradually they drew level with the house. Domenic's father greeted them. "Have you traveled far?"

"All the way from Cassino," the woman in the lead said. "The town was shelled and we took refuge in the monastery. Then the monastery itself was bombed."

Signore Luppino stared at them. "Mother of God! They bombed the Abbey of Monte Cassino!"

"Many, many bombs," the woman said. "As if they would wipe it from the face of the earth."

"Bombed the monastery," Signore Luppino repeated, "but why?"

The woman shrugged. "Who knows the ways of generals?"

Standing shyly behind his father, Domenic's eyes rested on the girl with the bandage around her head. Despite the bandage and the mud-caked clothes and the exhaustion written on her face, he thought she was the most beautiful girl he'd ever seen. That she was several years older than him only made her more alluring, more unapproachable. She noticed him staring, and he blushed, quickly looking away.

"My name is Rossi," he heard the woman, who seemed to be the leader, tell his father. "We've been traveling for many days. Could you spare some water and a bit of food?"

"Of course. Forgive me, Signora Rossi. Here I am asking questions while you stand there thirsty and hungry.

You are welcome to drink from our well, but . . . ," he hesitated, "I fear we don't have much food." He raised his arms and let them drop in despair. "The German soldiers, you know, taking, taking, always taking from the farmers. . . . But come, we will share what we have."

"*Grazie,* you are very kind."

While Domenic worked the pump, the refugees gathered around the well, refilling the battered metal cup again and again. When at last they had drunk their fill, Domenic's mother led them into the house.

In the kitchen, she buzzed around, giving them bread and soup and making them as comfortable as she could. Domenic watched as his mother gently unwound the rag on the young boy's shoulder, exposing an ugly gash.

"*Povero bambino,*" she said, as she bathed the wound. The boy flinched slightly at the touch of the hot water, but said nothing.

"How did it happen?" Domenic asked.

"A shell," he said laconically, his face impassive, as if it was an everyday event.

Signora Rossi explained. "After we left the monastery, we had to pass by a German artillery battery. They were shelled by the Allies and one shell exploded near us. A piece of shrapnel went into Sergio's shoulder. I pulled it out and bandaged it as best I could." Domenic shuddered as he imagined how much it must have hurt.

The same explosion had injured the girl. "Knocked Adriana right out," Signora Rossi said. "A concussion, I suspect."

The woman with the crutch took up the story. "Rocks were flying all around us. One hit me on the leg. It cracked my kneecap."

"A wonder you weren't all killed," Signora Luppino said.

There was a silence and the refugees looked at the floor. "Two of us were," Signora Rossi said quietly. "We carried their bodies until we came to a place where there was enough earth to dig graves. We had only a tin pot to dig with, but managed."

"Let me see your head," Signora Luppino said to Adriana. She unwound the rag, parted the hair, and examined her scalp. She cleaned it, then tore up an old dress and used the strips to bandage both Adriana's and Sergio's wounds.

Signore Luppino, meanwhile, was asking about the battle at Monte Cassino. "How much longer can the Germans hold out there?"

Signora Rossi shrugged. "Who knows? The fighting on the mountain goes on and on." She shook her head. "All the killing; terrible. We saw many bodies – from both sides. And so young."

"But the Allies will take Monte Cassino, surely," Signore Luppino said. "It will all be over soon, won't it?"

Signora Rossi pursed her lips doubtfully. "Many armies have attacked Monte Cassino, but in fourteen centuries not one has been able to capture it." She shook her head. "My husband, before they took him away, said they will be fighting there for a long time yet."

Signore Luppino groaned.

⌘

The next morning, Domenic's mother served up what she could for breakfast – a bit of soup, and a small portion of bread for each. The refugees ate eagerly. "You are very kind to share your food with us," Signora Rossi said.

Domenic managed to sit beside Adriana. She ate quietly, seeming lost in thought. He wanted to talk to her, to say something that would interest her, but he couldn't think of anything, so he stayed silent.

On the other side of him, the young boy with the wounded shoulder, Sergio, demolished his bread in one mouthful.

Domenic slipped his piece onto Sergio's empty plate. Sergio looked up. "Don't you want it?"

"I'm not hungry," he said. "You take it."

"That was nice of you," Adriana whispered, and he burned with pleasure.

Domenic's mother took down the large metal tub she used for washing clothes. "Bring in lots of water, Domenic," she said.

He lugged in pail after pail of water, while Signora Rossi collected the dirt-encrusted clothes from the refugees, passing out an assortment of old clothes and blankets for them to wear in the meantime.

Soon the clothesline behind the house was full of tattered but clean dresses, pants, and shirts. The overflow was spread out on rocks and bushes. "Let's hope they dry before it rains," Signora Luppino said.

The sun peeked out briefly, warming up the day. Sergio, bandaged shoulder and all, made high arcs on the swing, while Domenic climbed to his usual perch in the oak tree. Adriana sat on a rock watching Dolce munch on the brown winter grass and thought about Antonio with his mules, climbing the dangerous mountain trail night after night. Here the war seemed far away. How she wished that they could be together in a peaceful valley like this.

A small plane appeared over the mountains and dipped into the valley. It circled overhead.

Young Sergio jumped off the swing. "Come down!" he called to Domenic. "Quick!"

Domenic looked at the boy's worried, upturned face. He smiled. "But it's not a bomber, Sergio." He often saw the big bombers flying over at high altitudes on their way to attack the German supply lines in the north. "It's only a small plane."

"Come down," Sergio insisted. He seemed agitated. "Get in the house."

Domenic remained perched in the tree. Sergio looked up at him with eyes wise beyond his years. "Don't you know? The little plane tells the guns where to shoot. One flew over our town just before the shells came."

"But there aren't any Germans here to shoot at," Domenic said. Just then he heard a far-off, thunderlike rumble.

"It's the guns. Hurry!" Sergio was running now, calling to him over his shoulder. The other refugees were on the move too, rushing toward the house.

As Domenic climbed quickly down, he heard a whining noise, faint at first then growing louder, until it became a piercing scream. He reached the lowest branch and leaped off.

KABOOM! The shell exploded in the field, throwing up a fountain of earth. Paralyzed with fright, he stayed rooted to the spot. The whine of another shell jarred him into action and he ran for the house. Out of the corner of his eye, he saw Dolce galloping away.

He slammed the door behind him as a second explosion shook the house. Clumps of debris thumped against the wall; a window shattered, glass splinters flying. His father was herding everyone into the cellar.

More explosions followed in quick succession. Crouched in the cellar, the refugees, veterans of shelling, waited resignedly. The Luppino family, experiencing this horror of war for the first time, huddled together in shock.

The shelling stopped abruptly. Heads were raised cautiously. "Is it over?" a small voice asked.

"Wait a bit longer," someone said.

They listened, tensed for more explosions. None came, but the distant rumble of guns could still be heard.

"They've found another target," one of the old men said. "We'd better bring in the washing quickly, while we have the chance."

"The washing!" Signore Luppino exclaimed. "Why worry about the washing at a time like this?"

The old man turned to him. "But don't you see? Our clothes were spread all over the garden. So many people in one farmhouse; the scout plane must have thought there were German troops here. Why else would they waste shells on a farmer and his family?"

"I'm sorry we brought this on you," Signora Rossi said.

They filed up from the cellar and went outside to inspect the damage. Chunks of stucco had been knocked off the side of the house, but no major harm done.

Domenic saw Dolce at the far end of the field, staring back at the house, ears erect, and he went to her and calmed her. Then he led her back to the garden.

Adriana joined them. "Poor Dolce. Is she all right?"

He nodded. "She was frightened by the noise."

Domenic watched her hand as it stroked Dolce's muzzle gently. He couldn't bring himself to look directly at her. What do you say to such a beautiful older girl? *I hope you'll stay here with us for a while? Do you have a boyfriend in Cassino?* He rejected these as silly. Of course a girl like Adriana would have a boyfriend. In the end, he turned and walked back toward the house.

He stopped and picked up a piece of shrapnel from the grass. Running his finger along the sharp edges of the triangle of metal, he thought, *This piece of steel was part of a shell made in a factory across the sea. It was sent to Italy on a ship, loaded on a truck, driven from the coast, loaded into a gun, and fired at our house from many miles away. Hard to believe.*

In the kitchen, his mother was preparing the food for the airmen. Domenic knew it was time for his daily trip to the old mill. But today there was a problem, for young Sergio followed him wherever he went, looking up to him as if he were the older brother he had lost.

Not that Domenic minded him being around – he liked Sergio – but it had been drummed into him that no one, not even his young sisters, must know about the airmen hiding in the mill. Somehow he must make the trip today without Sergio.

Saying Good-bye

12

*D*omenic's mother handed him the bowl. She had told the visitors that he was taking the food to his aunt in the village.

"I lied to them," she said guiltily. "I'll have to go to confession and ask forgiveness for my sin." Domenic thought it best not to mention that he'd felt no guilt whatsoever when he told the very same lie to the German soldier who had stopped him – just relief that the soldier believed him. Did that mean he was a sinner?

He tried to slip out the door without Sergio seeing him, but he'd barely started across the field when the boy came running after him, his one good arm pumping. "Wait, Domenic," he panted. "I'll come with you."

Domenic saw the expectant look on his face. He knew he had to send him back, but hated to hurt his feelings.

"A German patrol may stop me and ask questions," he said. "It can be dangerous."

But Sergio stayed by his side, taking quick steps to keep up with Domenic's longer ones. "We saw lots of German soldiers when we were leaving the monastery," he said.

"Weren't you scared?"

"One of them gave me an orange." He grinned, remembering its juiciness. "It was really good."

This isn't working, thought Domenic. *I can't let him come to the old mill. I'll have to be tough.*

He stopped and faced the boy. "I'm sorry, Sergio . . . I want to go alone. You can't come."

For a moment, Sergio stood stock-still. Then his eyes filled with tears and he wheeled quickly and ran back to the house.

Domenic sighed and plodded on across the field. He reached the mill without incident.

The airmen had heard the shells exploding and were full of questions. "What's happened?" Jerome asked. "Big noise." He covered his ears to show what he meant. "*Boom. Boom.* Have our soldiers come?"

Domenic tried his best to explain. He mimicked the flight of a shell with his hand, level at first then plunging downward. He finished by throwing both hands in the air like an explosion.

"Airplanes?" Harry guessed. "Bombs?"

Domenic shook his head.

The airmen exchanged puzzled looks. "Like a ruddy game of charades," Harry said.

Again, Domenic mimicked the flight of a shell.

"Artillery shells!" Harry said suddenly. "That's what he means."

"But what were they shooting at?" Jerome wondered aloud. "Soldiers? German soldiers . . . here?"

Again Domenic shook his head. "No soljers."

"What then? What were they shooting at?"

Domenic hesitated. How could he explain about the refugees, and the laundry on the bushes, and the scout plane? It was all too difficult. He shrugged and lifted his hands palms up.

"Must have been a mistake," Jerome said. "Wrong target. It happens."

"And here I thought the good old British army had finally arrived," Harry said. He sighed. "Oh, well, back to waiting." He picked up the bowl and, draping a rag over his arm like a waiter, held it out to Jerome. "Champagne with your lunch today, sir?"

Domenic again thought how strange these Englishmen were.

On the way back home, he passed the creek where he had built his dam the day the German soldier with the dog had questioned him. Some of the stones he had used to make his dam were still there. That gave him an idea.

When he arrived back at the farmhouse, he found Sergio sitting on the floor by the hearth, his head down.

"*Ciao,* Sergio," he said. "I'm back."

No answer.

He crouched beside the boy. "Like to go play in the creek?"

Sergio looked up. "The creek?"

"There's a creek on the other side of the field. We could build a dam."

Sergio pushed himself up with his good arm and rolled to his feet. "Okay," he said, already halfway to the door, and they raced out together and spent the afternoon happily rebuilding the dam.

⌘

That night, Signora Rossi and the other refugees came to a decision.

"We think it best if we leave tomorrow," she said to the Luppinos. "You have been very generous, but we must not use up any more of your food."

Signora Luppino assured her they were welcome to stay; but inwardly, though she was ashamed to admit it, she was relieved. She had lain awake in the night, worrying about using up the food they had left. Still, she would miss the companionship of Signora Rossi, Adriana, Sergio, and the others. "Where will you go?" she asked.

"To Adriana's relative," Signora Rossi said. "We met a farmer one day who knew him and told us how to get there." She named a valley to the north. "It's still a long way, but now we know where we are going. Bless you for your help, and may we meet again when this war is over."

When the refugees set out the next morning, the whole Luppino family came with them to the road to wave good-bye. Long after the others had returned to the house, Domenic continued to watch the little band. Their figures grew smaller and smaller until they faded from sight.

They'll have a hard time crossing the mountains, he thought. He wished he was going with them – to help young Sergio and the others, but mainly to be with Adriana. He turned away. If only he were older.

As he was returning to the house, he heard the whine of laboring engines. Something was coming over the hill. He stopped to see what it was. A camouflaged truck appeared, grew larger, and rocketed past. The back was full of German soldiers. A second truck packed with soldiers followed.

He saw his father pause in the act of stacking firewood, and his brother, Guido, lean on his ax to stare after the trucks.

That afternoon, Domenic's aunt sent a message to her sister that the Germans were searching houses in the village and taking men for labor. "They will search the farms too," the message said. "Your husband and Guido must hide."

That night, Domenic's father sat him down and explained that he and Guido would have to leave.

"Where will you go?"

"You remember the hut in the hills?" Papa said. Domenic nodded; he remembered being there once many years ago. "We will hide out there. We leave tomorrow."

Domenic winced. His father and Guido gone! Just Mama and him, and his little sisters. Alone. With German troops all around them.

"You will have to be the man of the house, Domenic," his father said.

The man of the house! There it was. He'd known it was coming, whatever it meant, but he'd pushed it to the back of his mind. Now he would have to face it squarely.

"But what about the airmen, Papa?" With more German soldiers in the valley, could he still make the trip to the old mill to take food to them?

"The old mill is no longer safe," his father said. "We'll take them with us. Tomorrow will be your last trip to the mill."

Domenic felt a surge of relief; yet he would miss seeing the airmen every day.

"When you go tomorrow, tell them we'll come to get them. As soon as it's dark."

"But —" How could he possibly make them understand all that?

"You must learn the words in their language," his father, who spoke some English, said. "Try it now. Say 'tonight.'"

"Too-nite."

"'Papa come tonight.' Say it."

"Papa cum too-nite."

"Good. Practice that now."

⌘

As he made his way to the mill for the last time, Domenic said the English words over and over. At the mill entrance, he hesitated, suddenly anxious. What if they didn't understand? Would they just look at him and laugh? He said the strange words one more time, then pushed open the door and went inside.

When the airmen greeted him, Domenic, wanting to get it over, took a deep breath and plunged in.

"Soljers," he said. What was the word for "many"? He should have asked Papa. Then he remembered the hand signals used at the auctions in town that his father took him to before the war, and he held up the fingers of both hands, made a fist, then opened up his fingers again. He repeated this several times. *"Molti,"* he said.

The airmen looked at him intently. "Many soldiers! *Tedesco?*"

Domenic nodded.

"Damn," Harry swore. "German soldiers."

"Bad news," Jerome said.

"Too-nite," Domenic said loudly, to get their attention.

Their heads swiveled back to him. "What?"

"Papa cum too-nite."

He saw them look at each other, frowning. "Why is his father coming tonight?" Jerome said, puzzled.

"Maybe it's too dangerous to hide us any longer," Harry said. "Maybe he's coming to tell us to leave."

"Maybe," Jerome agreed. "But what do we do now?"

Their words were just babble to Domenic, but somehow he knew they hadn't understood. He had no more English words; he'd have to show them. He stared at the floor, thinking.

Suddenly he realized he was looking at the answer – the layer of dusty grain that covered the floor. He knelt and drew a picture in the dust with his finger. They watched intently as he pointed to his drawing and then to the walls of the mill.

"Okay, that's a picture of the mill," Harry said. "So?"

Domenic then drew four stick figures walking away from the mill. He pointed to the first two stick figures. "Papa, Guido," he said. Then he pointed to the last two figures and to the two men leaning over him. "Too-nite," he said again.

"Ah, now I get it," Jerome said.

"That's us." said Harry. "Seems like we're leaving tonight with his father, and someone called Guido."

Domenic drew another picture – a small hut surrounded by hills.

"They're taking us to another hideout," Jerome said.

Domenic knew they had understood. He got up to go. The airmen shook his hand and patted him on the back and tried to thank him with their few words of Italian. *"Grazie, Domenic. Mille grazie! Ciao, Domenic."*

He crossed to the door. *"Arrivederci, signori,"* he said. Then he went out, his job accomplished.

The Captain

13

*D*omenic was uneasy. Without his father or his brother, the house felt different. Noises in the night, noises he'd paid no attention to before, now woke him – the floorboards creaking as the house got colder, the loose shutter rattling, rain beating against the windows, the wind moaning in the oak tree, Dolce braying. He would lie there, listening, his imagination conjuring up an intruder creeping through the house. He told himself he should get up and investigate, but it was scary feeling his way around the house in the dark. And what would he do if he did encounter an intruder? It was a relief when morning arrived and he saw that the house hadn't been broken into, nor Dolce taken from her shed.

During the day, it was better. He was busy – bringing in wood to keep the fire going, fetching water, and doing other chores for his mother. He looked after Dolce, bringing her hay, and brushing her.

He liked brushing Dolce, found it reassuring somehow. A routine that comforted him as much as it did her. "Everything's going to be all right, Dolce," he would say, as he ran the brush through her thick brown coat. "The war will be over someday. Then we'll have lots of good things to eat, and sugar lumps for you again."

Then, too, there was the reassuring presence of his mother. He missed his father, but, all in all, being the man of the house wasn't so bad.

Yet, one day, everything changed.

⌘

A long line of German trucks, tanks, motorcycles, jeeps, and staff cars wound its way like a snake into the valley.

Domenic heard them long before they reached the farm. As the convoy drew closer, he saw that some of the trucks were hauling antiaircraft guns; others were piled high with equipment; still others, jammed with soldiers. The roar of engines filled the valley.

Mama ran out to the end of the lane, where he was gaping at the sight. She seized his arm. "In the house, Domenic, quickly!" Then she ran to the garden, where Angela and Pia were playing, and hurried them inside.

They waited in the kitchen, listening tensely as the convoy thundered past. Suddenly they heard the squeal of brakes in the lane . . . a shouted order . . . footsteps. The door burst open and a captain strode in, followed by two soldiers with rifles raised and a lieutenant.

Hands on his hips, the captain surveyed the house, ignoring the family clutching each other in the kitchen. His high, polished boots shone in the light from the open doorway. He slapped his leg with his swagger stick and nodded affirmatively to the lieutenant.

Noting the stairs leading to the second floor, the captain took them two at a time. When he came back down, he gave an order. The lieutenant saluted smartly, and went out to a waiting truck.

Signora Luppino marched boldly toward the captain. "What are you doing in my house?"

The two soldiers moved to block her way. Domenic held his breath, but the captain motioned the soldiers back. "Your house is required by the army, Signora," he said curtly, in perfect Italian. Then he mounted the stairs again.

The family heard his footsteps overhead and an order called down. The two soldiers hurried up the stairs. From above came the screech of something heavy being dragged across the floor. This was followed by grunts, then a loud crash from outside.

Through the open door, Domenic saw his mother's ancient chest of drawers hit the ground. The top split and the drawers spilled out. Her pride and joy, the chest was a family heirloom. The framed pictures of her mother and father followed the chest.

She screamed and rushed to the door. A soldier pushed by her into the house, lugging a heavy shortwave radio. Another followed, buried under an armload of maps.

Domenic could only watch. He felt he should do something, but the burly soldiers intimidated him. His mother started up the stairs, a determined look on her face. He knew her temper. "Mama, don't!" he warned, but she kept going. He took a deep breath and went to join her.

At the top of the stairs, a soldier motioned them back. When his mother ignored him, the soldier hefted his rifle and pointed it.

"In my own house!" she cried. But there was nothing to do but retreat.

For the next hour, soldiers hurried in and out, carrying tables, chairs, transmitters, blackboards, cots, and other paraphernalia. They threw out whatever of the family's belongings were in their way.

Domenic and his mother stayed in the kitchen, wondering what was to happen. Shy Pia, her eyes wide, peered from behind her mother's skirt. Angela, the bolder one, looked hard at the intruders who had dared to move into their house.

Eventually the traffic in and out of the house slowed, and the soldiers lounged by the stairs, waiting for further orders.

The captain came down and the men scrambled to their feet. When he noticed the family watching him, the captain strode to the kitchen. A tall lanky man, militarily erect in bearing, he towered over them. They looked up, Domenic apprehensive, his mother defiant.

"I will use the upstairs for my headquarters; my soldiers will be billeted downstairs," the captain said bluntly.

Domenic shuddered. He visualized sleeping outside in the cold and rain.

His mother opened her mouth to protest, but the captain stopped her. "As long as you don't interfere, Signora, you and your children may stay here, but in the kitchen only, you understand." He turned to leave. "And kindly keep out of our way."

Domenic glanced at his mother. She gave a helpless shrug. "What can we do?" she said, once the captain had left, and went back to peeling a wizened potato.

For the rest of the morning he stayed close to his mother, listening to the tramp of boots in and out of the house. He was relieved they would still have a roof over their heads; at the same time he dreaded having German soldiers right here in the house.

At noon, the men came into the kitchen and used the fireplace to heat their rations. Signora Luppino herded her family into the far corner. Most of the soldiers ignored them, but Domenic noticed one in particular staring at them. He was the one he'd heard the soldiers call Corporal; his eyes were full of hate.

That night the family slept on blankets on the kitchen floor, cold and hard, but Mama wouldn't hear of complaints. "Think of your father and your brother," she said. "They'll be colder and hungrier than we are. I only thank God they left in time."

Domenic slept fitfully. Snores and grunts and belches from the other rooms reminded him that soldiers were sprawled all over the house. A guard had been posted outside the front door, and he heard the murmur of voices when the relief took over, and smelled their cigarettes.

During the day, most of the soldiers were working or training outside. In the lane, a staff car, a jeep, and a motorcycle sat waiting, and at intervals a dispatch rider, leather pouch slung over his shoulder, hurried down the stairs and out the door. From the kitchen window, Domenic would watch him leap on the motorcycle, crank the starter pedal, and speed away. When he came back, the rider would rush up the stairs, the pouch flapping against his hip.

If he had to become a soldier someday, Domenic thought, that would be the job he wanted.

By the end of the day, though, the motorcycle, plastered with dung-colored mud, looked like a different machine from the shiny black one that had sat in the lane in the morning; and the rider, two circles like owl's eyes where his goggles had been, would climb the stairs wearily.

Sometimes the motorcycle chugged back down the lane with bullet holes in its fenders, sometimes with the driver's leg or arm bandaged; sometimes the machine didn't come back at all and the lane sat empty – except for the staff car and the jeep, which appeared lonely, as if they missed their companion. The next day, a replacement motorcycle would show up with a new driver.

Sometimes the lieutenant would come down the stairs after a briefing and set out briskly cross-country, accompanied by two or three soldiers. The soldiers wore backpacks, their rifles slung over their shoulders; grenades, bayonets, and water bottles hanging from their belts. The lieutenant wore a pistol in a shiny leather holster, and carried a map. Domenic saw that they always went in the same direction – toward the enemy lines, he supposed. Before leaving, the men would cluster around the officer, peering at the map.

When they came back, a few days later, they would be walking slowly and methodically, like robots, faces drawn. The officer would disappear up the stairs with the map, and Domenic would hear the radio transmitter crackle into life.

Once, the lieutenant returned alone and bedraggled.

Another time, just a lone soldier came back to make the slow climb up the stairs with the map. A new lieutenant arrived to take the other's place.

In the Luppinos' fields, soldiers wheeled large guns into position and erected nets over them, covering the nets with branches and leaves until they blended into the surroundings. Some of the guns pointed straight up at the sky, others at an angle toward the enemy lines. Italian civilians in ragged clothes, with haunted expressions, labored in the fields under guard, digging pits and hauling buckets of cement to construct bunkers.

⌘

One day, the captain came down the stairs, stretching and rubbing his eyes. He paced the front room, muttering to himself. When he saw Domenic watching from the kitchen, he went over to him.

"So, young man, are my soldiers treating you all right?"

Domenic bent and poked the fire. He nodded shyly. *"Si, Capitano."*

"What is your name?"

"Domenic," he said, keeping his eyes on the fire.

"And how old are you, Domenic? No, wait. . . ." The captain held up his hand. "Don't tell me. Let me guess. Stand up."

Domenic straightened up. He shifted uneasily, self-conscious under the captain's steady gaze. Mama stopped her work and watched nervously.

"You are . . . *hmm,* let me see . . . thirteen," he pronounced finally.

Domenic started. "H-How did you know that, Captain?"

"Easy. My son is fourteen now, but the last time I saw him he was thirteen and just your size."

Despite his awe of the captain, Domenic had to ask, "What is your son's name?"

"Gunther. He's named after my father. He wrote me a letter. It came today." The pride in the captain's voice was apparent. He took the letter from the pocket of his tunic and smoothed it out. "Would you like to hear what he said?" Without waiting for an answer, he began to read.

"'*Leiber Vati.*' That means Dear Papa," he interjected.

"'We got your letter about your long train trip and Mama read it to us over and over. I am glad you are well. I go to a different school now as our old school was hit by a bomb. It is quite a long walk, but I don't mind. There is an empty field beside the school where we play soccer. I scored a goal yesterday.

"'Mama is out now. She has to line up to buy bread, and I am looking after little Katerina. I have a lot of homework for my science class, so I'd better go. Mama is writing to you too and I'll put my letter in the same envelope. I hope you get it soon and that everything is all right wherever you are, Papa. We talk about you a lot. Your son, Gunther. P.S. Next time you come home, maybe you will watch me play soccer.'"

The captain folded the letter and stared into the fire.

"It's a very nice letter," Domenic said. The captain looked so melancholy, he was emboldened to go on. "It's hard to write letters. I never know what to say."

The captain nodded. "And it's especially hard to write letters to a father who is always away." He put the letter back in his pocket, then walked briskly out of the kitchen.

The Grenade   *14*

The next time Domenic saw him, the captain was
climbing into the staff car with the lieutenant. He
watched wistfully as the car disappeared down the road.
Without the captain, who knew how they would be
treated? He longed to know if he was coming back, but
couldn't look to see if his belongings were still upstairs;
there was always a guard at the top.

That night, when the soldiers filed in from their
duties, they were more boisterous than usual. The corporal motioned to one of the soldiers and the two of them
clumped down the cellar stairs. They came back up with
bottles of the wine that Domenic's father had made. The
corporal brushed roughly past Domenic and set the bottles
down by the hearth.

More soldiers drifted into the kitchen, eyeing the

wine. The corporal uncorked a bottle and took a long gulp. The family retreated quietly into a corner.

The wine was passed around amid singing, shouted toasts, and the clink of bottles. A ruddy-faced young soldier cheerfully lifted his glass toward the corner where Domenic, his mother, and his sisters were keeping very still. *"Vino buono,"* the young soldier called, smiling. Domenic mustered a tentative smile in response, but his mother remained stone-faced.

One of the soldiers produced some eggs. Another raided the bin where Signora Luppino kept her small supply of bread. Domenic grimaced as the remaining bread disappeared. The corporal gave an order, and two soldiers went outside and returned with armfuls of firewood from the Luppinos' dwindling woodpile. Dipping chunks of bread in egg, the soldiers fried them over a roaring fire.

The bottles were refilled from the barrel in the cellar. At first, all seemed in the spirit of fun, but soon arguments began. One soldier pushed another and a fight broke out. The sergeant came downstairs and stopped it with a sharp command.

More wine was fetched. The corporal handed a bottle to the sergeant, who disappeared back upstairs with it. Domenic was sorry to see him go.

The party became noisier. The corporal pointed at the Luppinos and said something that brought a burst of laughter. Domenic's heart skipped a beat when he motioned to them to come by the fire. He didn't trust the corporal; didn't want to go anywhere near him.

His mother shook her head, but the corporal was insistent. He held out his hands, as if warming them over the fire. *"Kommen Sie,"* he said.

Again Domenic's mother shook her head, but the corporal wasn't taking no for an answer. He stood over them, motioning that they were to move to the fire. Signora Luppino refused to look at him, and Domenic kept his eyes on the floor.

Still the corporal persisted until, finally, Signora Luppino sighed, took the girls by the hand, and moved to the fireplace with Domenic. They settled nervously.

One of the soldiers amused Angela and Pia by making funny faces; another created rabbit silhouettes on the wall with his hands. Angela giggled. Even Pia, peeking shyly from behind her mother, smiled.

At least it's warm by the fire, Domenic thought. Maybe the corporal wasn't so bad after all; maybe he only wanted to share the fire with them. Yet, as Domenic snuck a furtive look at the corporal tipping back the wine bottle and then belching and glowering at them, he knew he didn't.

As if to prove him right, the corporal chose that moment to disappear into the front room. When he came back, he had something in his hand, which he held up to show them. It was a gray cylindrical object, with a long wooden throwing handle extending from the bottom.

Domenic flinched. He knew immediately what it was. He'd seen the German-style grenades hanging from the soldiers' belts when they left for missions to the south.

Beside him, he heard his mother gasp.

The corporal laughed drunkenly. The other soldiers scrambled to get out of the way.

Domenic's mother screamed. She grabbed the girls and tried to leave, but the corporal blocked her way. He made as if to throw the grenade into the fire. She seized the opportunity to rush by him to the door, sweeping the girls along with her. Domenic was only a step behind. The corporal's insane laughter followed them outside.

They stood uncertainly in the dark, half-expecting to hear the grenade explode at any moment. Domenic tried to comfort his sisters. "He was only trying to scare us."

"He's crazy drunk," Mama said. "He might do anything."

It began to rain. Domenic shivered. "Maybe he'll fall asleep soon," he said, hopefully, "and we can go back."

But his mother was having no more of the drunken corporal. "We're staying out here," she said. "I'd rather freeze than be blown up by that madman."

Domenic's teeth chattered. "Couldn't we go to Aunt's house in the village?"

"Not at night. There are soldiers everywhere."

The kitchen door opened and a chorus of "Lilli Marlene" spilled out. The family retreated around a corner of the house as a soldier lurched out and relieved himself, bellowing the song into the rain.

When the door slammed behind him, Domenic's mother took the girls by the hand. "We will not spend the rest of the night here watching that sort of thing. Come, girls, Domenic." And off she marched.

Domenic hurried after her. He slipped and fell in a puddle, then got up again. Where was she going?

Mama didn't stop until she reached a rickety shed, which canted at an angle like a drunkard. As she unlatched the door, Domenic thought, *Oh, no, not the old henhouse.* The hens were long gone, but the smell of their droppings lingered, and the roof leaked. "Why not Dolce's shed?" he said. "It's dry."

"No room," his mother said curtly, "with Dolce and my chest of drawers in there." She and Domenic had managed to drag the chest, from where it had been thrown the day the Germans moved in, over to Dolce's shed.

She shooed them all inside the henhouse. As he heaped up straw for their beds, Domenic was glad it was dark so he couldn't see the dried chicken droppings in it.

Mama hugged the girls to her for warmth. Domenic lay close beside her, shivering and listening to raucous sounds from the house, until he finally fell asleep.

The Punishment 15

*D*omenic woke early to find himself snuggled up against his mother's back for warmth. He pulled away, embarrassed. She stirred, and the girls, sleeping in her arms, whimpered.

Light filtered in through the cracks in the henhouse. He got up and peeked out the door. The farmhouse sat still and silent, as if recovering its dignity.

He clutched himself for warmth; his empty stomach gurgled. "Can we go back now, Mama?" he ventured. No answer.

A door slammed, echoing in the calm morning air, and he heard voices. Peering out, he saw soldiers slouching morosely, some leaning against the house smoking, one down on his knees retching. The sergeant and the corporal

115

came out, orders were barked, and the men formed work details and marched off.

"We can go back now, Mama," Domenic said. "The soldiers have left for the day."

His mother opened her eyes. "All right, but you must build up the fire for Angela. She's caught a bad cold." She and Domenic carried the girls back to the house, Angela coughing and shivering. Mama took the girls inside.

When Domenic approached the woodpile behind the house, he saw that the soldiers had used up most of their carefully shepherded firewood. He gathered up what he could from the remains and restarted the fire.

His mother surveyed their depleted food supply, shaking her head in dismay. "You'll have to go out and collect dandelions, Domenic. There's hardly anything left to cook."

Domenic was about to remind her that there were still the pots of food buried in the field, until he realized they couldn't risk digging up even one pot – not with German soldiers around. They would take it, and all the other pots too, once they found out about them. The food might as well be on the moon.

He spent the morning roaming the fields, looking for dandelions, staying well away from the guns and bunkers where the soldiers were. He had to go to the edge of the far woods, but, eventually, he filled his sack. As he was walking back to the house, he saw the staff car pull into the lane and the captain step out.

Rushing into the kitchen, he shouted, "Good news, Mama. The captain's back!"

His mother looked up and a slow smile spread over her worn features. How long it had been since he'd seen his mother smile. "Thank the Lord for that," she said. "We'll sleep safely tonight."

Angela was hunched by the fireplace, coughing – a long, hacking cough. Domenic patted her head and added the remaining bits of wood to the fire. He wondered if he could chop down a tree, drag it back to the house, and split it up, like his father and Guido did. Tomorrow, he'd have to try.

"Is your sister not well, Domenic?" a voice said.

He looked up. The captain was standing in the doorway.

"She caught cold from being out in the rain last night," he said.

"Out in the rain?"

Dare I tell him what happened? Domenic wondered. *If I do, will the corporal take revenge on us next chance he gets?*

His mother appeared from the cellar, some scraps of potatoes in her hand. "It was a bad night for us, Captain," she said.

Unlike Domenic, his mother had no compunction about telling what happened. The captain listened, his eyes flashing as the story unfolded.

"That will never happen again, I assure you," he said. He strode to the front door and they heard him calling the sergeant, who appeared promptly, saluted, and followed the captain up the stairs.

The captain's raised voice reverberated throughout the house. Soon the sergeant rushed down and out the door. He returned a few minutes later, followed by the corporal. They mounted the stairs, heads down.

That night the house was quiet, the soldiers subdued.

⌘

The next morning, Domenic was at the well when he saw the corporal come out of the house. He was carrying his backpack, a bedroll draped over the top like a limp body. Grenades dangled from his belt and a submachine gun was slung over his shoulder. He climbed into the back of the jeep and sat glowering. When his eyes met Domenic's, he stared at him maliciously. Domenic quickly dropped his gaze. He didn't look up until the jeep was accelerating out of the lane, the corporal a dark shape in the back.

Was the corporal coming back? If he did, he would make their lives miserable. He remembered his grandmother's claim that throwing a coin in the well would make your wish come true. He had his old coin – he always carried it for luck – maybe now was the time to use it. It might save them all. He took it from his pocket and rubbed it.

Domenic held the coin over the well. "May the corporal never come back," he said – twice to make sure – then opened his fingers. He heard the coin *plunk* into the water below and carried the full pail into the kitchen.

"The captain was here," his mother said. "We will have no more trouble with the corporal. He's been sent to join the troops on Monte Cassino."

Relief swept over Domenic. Had his wish come true already?

"The captain said the sergeant was also to blame for falling asleep and not keeping order," his mother went on. "He's still here, but he has been disciplined."

Later, the sergeant came into the kitchen, followed by two soldiers with armfuls of fresh-cut wood. He said nothing, merely gestured curtly to the men to build up the fire. A faded spot on his sleeve showed where one of the chevrons of a sergeant had been removed; he had been demoted to corporal.

The Luppino family slept well that night.

In the morning, Domenic saw a truck wheel into the lane, towing the jeep the corporal had left in. It was riddled with bullet holes, its windshield shattered. A soldier came out of the house and lifted a backpack, with a bedroll on top, and a submachine gun from the jeep. He carried them into the house and set them down by the door.

Domenic saw that the backpack was bloodstained and pierced with small, round, black-edged holes – bullet holes. A terrible guilt swept over him. The corporal was not coming back, now or ever. His wish had been granted, but in a way he'd never imagined. . . .

He sighed, picked up his empty sack, and left in search of dandelions, unable to shake his guilt. For a long time afterwards, a mental image of the corporal's bloody body sprawled by the roadside haunted him.

The Mule Train

16

*A*ntonio stroked the soft white muzzle of his favorite mule. The first time he tried to get the mule moving, he hadn't known the secret. He thought the mule was just stubborn. "As stubborn as the dictator Mussolini himself," he'd muttered, as he vainly pulled on the lead. He named the mule Mussolini on the spot. He hadn't even noticed then that she was a mare, not a stallion as many of the pack mules were.

One of the other muleteers – a wizened farmer from the Liri Valley, wise in the ways of mules – had come to Antonio's rescue that first time. "I remember her," the old muleteer had said, pointing to the mule, who was holding up the entire train. "She's a bell mule, that one."

"A what?"

"A bell mule. She was trained to lead wearing a bell;

the other mules followed the sound." He snorted. "Can't wear a bell here, though. Every gun for miles around would be shooting at you. Still she's used to being the leader, bell or no bell, so let her."

"Thank you for telling me," Antonio'd said gratefully.

The old muleteer had gazed up at the mountain, looming over them in the gathering dusk. "Don't thank me. I'm not doing you, or her, any favors telling how to get her moving. Chances are none of us'll make many more trips up there before our luck runs out."

Antonio had quickly shifted the other mules he was responsible for, and put the one he'd called Mussolini in the lead. She started out with no further delay.

Small, but tough and determined, she plodded on through the night, no matter how steep and slippery and narrow the trail. In a way, she *was* like the dictator, he decided, determined to lead the others even if it was to their destruction. The name Mussolini stuck, though she had a sweet nature unlike that of the hotheaded dictator.

As he got to know her, Antonio felt they understood each other perfectly. She would gaze at him with her sad brown eyes as though she knew they both longed to be somewhere else – she among the olive groves and vineyards of the Liri Valley, he with Adriana far from the war.

Now it was time for yet another of their nightly treks.

⌘

As soon as it was dark enough to move without attracting artillery fire, the muleteers loaded their mules, under the supervision of German soldiers. Boxes of hand grenades and ammunition were strapped on first. Tonight there was, as well, a shipment of plate mines to go up the mountain.

Antonio hated loading plate mines. The mines were hung loosely from each side, and he'd seen what happened to a mule when a plate mine was hit by shrapnel and detonated.

After the ammunition, the grenades, and the mines, supplies for the troops were added – thermoses with lukewarm meals, bread, tea bags, sugar, candles, fuel for alcohol stoves, and bandages. Each mule could carry up to 100 kilos, tied on its back or slung balanced on either side. Sometimes, if there was room and the supply officer was in a good mood, a small ration of rum and some chocolate might be added.

The first group of mules led off. Antonio held Mussolini's halter, waiting their turn. When a soldier signaled to him, he gave the slight tug that was all Mussolini needed.

A drizzle of rain was falling, as it had off and on all day. *Another cold wet trip,* Antonio thought. Already, he was soaked through. How long had he been doing this? Weeks? Months? He'd lost count of the number of times he and his mules had struggled up the mountain, unloaded, then skidded and slipped back down again.

When he'd first been brought to the base camp, he thought only of escape. He was sure then that a chance would come to get away in the dark, especially when he saw how few soldiers went with the mule train. The Germans were chronically short of troops: Thousands of the casualties in Italy were not replaced because of the urgent need for men on the Russian front.

Two or three soldiers couldn't possibly watch all the muleteers. He'd thought it would simply be a matter of waiting for the right moment. He learned differently.

"German soldiers are all over the mountain," the old muleteer had warned him. "Some of those caves are big enough for a whole platoon of them. My brother tried to escape one night when we were halfway up. He got clear all right, looked like he was on his way. Then a machine gunner in one of the caves heard him. Guess he thought he was an enemy soldier." He sighed. "They have itchy trigger fingers up here at night. We found my brother's body on the next trip."

He shook his head forlornly. "Don't try it. If a German doesn't get you, an Allied sniper will."

With that, Antonio's dream of escaping and reuniting with Adriana dimmed. He knew he would feel badly abandoning Mussolini to her fate anyway. The next muleteer might treat her cruelly, taking out his anger at being conscripted by the Germans. He'd seen more than one doing that, beating his mules until the others stopped him.

Now he glanced back. Mussolini was methodically putting one hoof in front of the other, her head bobbing up and down with each step, the plate mines swinging back and forth below her belly. The quiet of the mountain was broken only by the *clip-clop* of hooves on rock and the urging of the muleteers. The rain turned to wet snow as they climbed higher.

The trail angled sharply upward, winding up a steep cliff, and the mules strained under their loads. Even Antonio, young as he was and with nothing to carry, found it hard going. He could hear the labored wheezing of the old muleteer behind him.

The rumble of Allied artillery broke out across the Liri Valley and, moments later, answering German artillery from the mountain. Flares shot up, turned the clouds green, then arced down. Bathed briefly in the sickly glow, the mule train plodded on.

A volley of shells shrieked over their heads. One landed just in front of the column, throwing up rocks and earth. Then, with a deafening roar, their world exploded.

The force of the blast knocked Antonio to the ground. He rolled into a hollow beside the path and covered his head. Detonation after detonation rang in his ears, like a string of giant firecrackers going off in sequence.

He shuddered as he realized what was happening. Some of the plate mines must have been hit, and each exploding mine set off others. A flying rock landed with a *thump* inches from his head.

The detonations petered out. Antonio waited, reluctant to raise his head for fear of what he would see. Then he heard the shouts of the other muleteers and the whinnies of mules in distress, and he scrambled to his feet.

One of his mules was lying in a pool of blood, motionless. Other mules were struggling to stand, helped by their muleteers. A guard was sprawled on his back across the path. Mussolini's white muzzle was nowhere to be seen.

Antonio peered over the brink of the incline. At the bottom, he saw Mussolini struggling to her feet. A blast had knocked her over the edge.

"Mussolini!" he called, but she hurdled a boulder and disappeared into the night, whinnying in terror. Antonio could hear her crashing through bushes.

He plunged down the incline, half-falling, half-sliding. Picking his way over the rocks, he tried to follow her. He'd chance the machine guns, he told himself, and when he caught up with her, they would both keep going, away from here forever.

On the Mountain   *17*

*A*ntonio paused in his headlong pursuit of Mussolini
to listen for her. Terrified by the shell blast that had
flung her from the path, she was plunging blindly on. The
surefooted mule could speed down the steep slopes much
faster than he could. Her frantic braying became more and
more faint.

He judged she was headed in the direction of an infa-
mous ridge that had changed hands several times in bloody
clashes, where the two sides were now separated by only a
ravine. He must stop her before she was shot at by one
side or the other. At night up here they shot at anything
that moved.

Stumbling after her, Antonio nearly walked off a cliff in
the dark. Recovering himself, he stopped to listen, but her
braying had faded away completely. He kept stubbornly on.

Suddenly, he heard voices nearby. He stopped dead. Then he heard Mussolini, somewhere close by, her quiet nicker a change from the terrified brays that had punctuated her flight. More like the noise she made when she was given a bit of sugar.

He moved cautiously toward the sound. Skirting some bushes, he saw bulky shapes ahead. As he crept closer, the shapes materialized into mules. Dim figures were unloading packs from the mules' backs. A voice spoke in a stage whisper, "Put it over here, chum."

The voice was speaking English!

Antonio was close enough now that he could see the soldiers' silhouettes. Their helmets were the shallow, rimmed helmets of Commonwealth soldiers; not the deep, "coal-scuttle" helmets of the Germans. He had stumbled on the Allied front line.

From the way they were keeping their voices low, he knew the German lines could not be far away.

"That's it then," he heard someone say. "Let's head back."

Antonio could understand some English; he'd picked it up from his grandfather when he came back from America. Even the accent he heard now was familiar – East Indian, like that of Signore Patel, who used to own the *pasticceria* in town before it was shelled.

"Lucky you, getting out of this hellhole," a voice

responded laconically. "Us poor buggers have to stay up here."

"But it's no fun for us either if we get caught on the trail in daylight," the first voice rejoined. "The Jerry gunners would use us for target practice. See you tomorrow night, chaps."

"God willing."

Antonio drifted closer as the mule train prepared to start the return trip. He mingled with the mules and soon picked out the white pattern of Mussolini's muzzle. An East Indian soldier was tugging vainly at her halter.

"Come on, move," the soldier pleaded. "We lucked out finding you, complete with a load of the Jerries' equipment, and now you won't move."

Antonio took a deep breath and spoke up as best he could in English. "She bell mule. Not follow, only lead."

"You know this one, do you?" The soldier peered at him. "Hey, where'd *you* come from?"

"Other side. . . . Got away. Try catch Mussolini."

The soldier shot him a quizzical glance. "Mussolini?"

Antonio stroked the white muzzle. "Her name Mussolini."

The soldier grinned. "I like it. What's *your* name?"

"Antonio."

"Let's go," someone farther back called, impatiently.

"Okay, then, Antonio, let's see you get this mule moving. She's holding up the line."

Antonio took her halter from the soldier. He gestured at the mules ahead of them. "Please to tell. . . ." He struggled to recall the English words. "Please to tell those mules go."

The soldier looked at him strangely, then shrugged and passed on the word. The front of the mule train moved off. Mussolini behaved exactly as Antonio said she would; as soon as the mules in front of her faded into the dark, she set out. The mules behind followed her lead.

The path down this side of the mountain turned out to be longer and steeper than that on the German side. As they descended, the snow of the higher altitude turned to freezing rain. Several times, Antonio's feet slipped out from under him and he had to grab Mussolini to keep from falling over the edge.

The sky began to lighten before the path finally flattened out and they reached a valley east of the town of Cassino. Antonio squinted into the distance at the remains of his town, still in German hands. He tried to pick out familiar landmarks, but it all looked the same now – rubble from one end to the other. He couldn't even tell where his house had been. Turning away, he felt his stomach churn.

The soldier who had first talked to him dropped back and walked alongside. "Want to work for us now, Antonio?

We'll pay you – not much, I admit, but you get your meals and that's worth more than money these days."

"*Si*," Antonio said, without hesitation. Why not? He would have stayed anyway to take care of Mussolini.

He knew he was far better off with the Allied side, which would treat him as a voluntary muleteer, not as forced labor. On the other hand, he was farther away from Adriana now. Between them lay the front lines; it was as if a steel door had been slammed shut, leaving her on one side of the battle and him on the other.

The possibility of escaping the Germans and finding Adriana again had been uppermost in his mind, nourishing his spirit. Now that he was with the Allied side, he could leave any time he wished – except that there was a new obstacle in his way: He would have to recross the German front lines to get to her.

At the base camp, Antonio and the other muleteers fed and watered the mules they'd been assigned. The men then headed toward the rocky hillside framing the valley.

Antonio stood watching them go, wondering if he should follow. They were much older than him, some the age his grandfather had been when he was killed, with the same worn, weather-beaten faces – the faces of men who'd worked in the fields all their lives.

One turned and beckoned. "Come with us, boy," he said.

The muleteers, it turned out, were living in the many natural caves dotting the hillside. "Protection from shells," one told him, succinctly. They were men of few words.

Antonio wandered the hillside until he found a small cave that hadn't been claimed. He piled rocks around the entrance to provide better protection – like the rock shelters he'd seen the troops on Mount Cassino build where there wasn't enough earth to dig.

He yawned. It had been a long night. He crawled into his cave and lay on the damp ground, shivering in his wet clothes. But with hunger pangs gnawing at his stomach, sleep was elusive and, eventually, he gave up. The soldier had mentioned something about meals, hadn't he?

Nearby, a muleteer was sitting cross-legged at the entrance to his cave, watching the rain. Antonio approached.

The muleteer continued to look into the distance.

He tried to think of something to say. "Are you from Cassino?"

The man shook his head and pointed. "From the north. They're still there – all by themselves."

"Who is?"

"My family. I couldn't stay. The Germans were seizing any man fit to work. But I should be there, helping my family. I don't even know if they're still alive."

"But you had to leave," Antonio said. "What else could you do?"

There was no response. The man continued to watch the rain. Antonio saw the pain in the man's eyes and understood why these men were so silent.

"One of the soldiers said something about meals," he ventured. "Can you tell me where to go? I haven't eaten since yesterday."

"I'll show you." The man got to his feet. "Soon be time."

Passing the field where the mules were grazing, they kept going until they reached an encampment of tents. Soldiers of the East Indian regiment were milling about, some lining up in front of a large tent from which emerged an aroma of spices. Those coming out were carrying plates of food and steaming cups.

"That's the cookhouse," the muleteer said. "We get ours after the soldiers." Antonio was glad to see that the line was moving fast.

"Hey, there, Antonio," a voice said in English. Surprised to hear his name, he looked around. A soldier was grinning at him. "How's Mussolini?"

Here was the soldier who'd offered him work as a muleteer. In the light of day, without his helmet, he looked much younger than he had last night on the mountain. *Only a few years older than me,* Antonio thought, *yet a veteran of war.* In a way, he was envious, though war was a nightmare of shells and death. Envious because the soldier belonged somewhere, was an integral part of something.

"Mussolini fine . . . sir," he added, like he'd heard them say in this army.

The soldier made a dismissive gesture. "Call me Vadin." He nodded toward the cookhouse, where the last of the line had now disappeared inside. "Your turn, if you're ready for some breakfast. Just rice and beans, but it's good and hot."

A hot meal sounded like heaven. Antonio drifted over, letting the older muleteers go ahead of him. They shuffled forward silently.

Inside, a soldier, stained apron over his uniform, ladled generous blobs of rice and beans onto plates. Antonio picked up a filled plate and a mug of hot rust-colored liquid and hurried out. He sat on the ground by Vadin and gobbled down half the plateful before he realized his mouth was on fire. Eyes watering, he was seized by a fit of coughing.

Vadin smiled and thumped his back. "The cook does go heavy on the curry powder. That's the way we like it. You'll get to like it too, I hope."

"Soon will," Antonio managed to say, before breaking out in another coughing fit. He picked up his mug and sniffed the reddish liquid cautiously. It was tea, very strong, but it soothed his burning mouth.

He finished his meal and checked on Mussolini before returning to his cave. There, warmed by the spicy food and hot tea, he slept deeply, waking just in time to load his mules for the nightly trek up the mountain.

The Camp

18

Night after night, the mule train set out to deliver supplies to the troops of the Indian regiment on the mountain, troops that never seemed to have enough ammunition, grenades, or food. Most nights, the muleteers were soaked through by the time they began the climb, as the low-hanging clouds enveloping the mountain dropped their loads of moisture – sometimes as rain, sometimes as snow.

Cold and miserable as those wet murky nights were, the occasional clear night was feared more. For on clear nights, especially those with a full moon, deadly accurate shelling rained down on the mule train. Those were the grimmest nights of all, and many mules and muleteers were lost to shell fire. So far, Antonio and Mussolini had been spared.

One day Antonio heard rumors circulating among the muleteers. Everyone seemed to know that something was about to happen, but no one knew what or when. Then, as he was perched on a rock by the cookhouse waiting for breakfast one morning, Vadin sat down beside him with the news.

The battle-weary Indian and New Zealand troops were finally being relieved, he said, relieved by Polish soldiers that had escaped from German-occupied Poland and formed a brigade to join the Allies. The Free Polish, they were called. This was their first assignment – a tough one too, Vadin said.

"I don't envy them. About bloody time we were relieved, though," he went on. "We're being sent to the rear for a rest. We'll still need the mules to carry our equipment; trucks aren't much use in this mud. And muleteers too, if you want to come along."

Antonio felt as if a burden had been lifted. He and Mussolini would no longer have to make the dreaded trip up the mountain every night. *Maybe now,* he thought, *maybe now would be the time to head northeast, in search of Adriana.*

He'd known her only a short time, yet he felt as if a part of him had been torn away when they were separated. Without her, something essential was missing from his life. First he'd lost his family, then Adriana. He would never again be with his family, but he might find Adriana. And find her he must, if he was ever to feel whole again.

But could he take Mussolini out from under the nose of the Indian battalion? he wondered. Whose mule was she, anyway? They probably considered Mussolini theirs, captured from the Germans.

But the biggest obstacle would be crossing the German front line. Odds were that he would be caught, and Mussolini, too, if she was with him. Once again they would be conscripted to work for the Germans.

Antonio sighed. He would just have to be patient. Wait, and hope the German army would soon be forced to retreat. Then he would be free to go in search of Adriana.

Vadin was looking at him, waiting for an answer.

"Yes, I come with you, sir . . . er, Vadin."

⌘

"Long way, this place," Antonio said. They had been walking for two days now. Not that he minded that; it was far better than making the dangerous trek up Monte Cassino every night. Here, well behind the Allied lines, no one was shooting at them.

"Not far now," Vadin said.

Most of the Indian troops were transported by army trucks, but the muleteers with their mules, and the Indians in charge, walked. They slogged all day through the goo, stirred up by months of winter rains.

Those in the trucks weren't having an easy time of it, either.

"Need a lift, lads?" Vadin called, as they filed past a truck bogged down in the mud. Its spinning tires were gleefully hurling globs of mud back at the soldiers trying to push. They scowled at Vadin.

Other trucks had slid completely off the road into the ditch and were hopelessly stuck. The mud-covered soldiers had given up pushing, and lounged against the truck smoking while they waited for a tow.

Occasionally a truck did roar by them – at full speed, to keep from bogging down. Then it was the turn of the soldiers in the back to jeer at the plodding mule train.

"It's like the tortoise and the hare," Vadin said. "We're slow, but we get there in the end." Though Antonio's understanding of English was improving every day, he had no idea what this meant. He gave Mussolini's muzzle a pat. "Be there soon, *mia amica.*"

When they eventually reached their destination, Antonio stared curiously around. They were in a valley, perhaps once green but now churned into a sea of mud by army vehicles. Remains of houses on either side of a shell-pocked road marked where a village had stood before the Allied offensive swept through. Blackened trunks of trees, like burnt fingers, pointed accusingly at the sky. "Look what you've done to our land," they seemed to say.

A scattering of khaki tents blended into the mud. Soldiers, some of them wearing turbans, drifted here and there among the tents.

The mules were led to a patch of brownish winter grass by the creek and turned loose to graze. Mussolini lifted her head and gave voice to a long drawn-out call, as if in celebration of their arrival. The call began like the whinnying of a horse, as mule calls do, and ended with the long drawn-out *hee-haw, hee-haw* of a donkey. Other mules joined in.

"Some rest camp," one of the Indian troopers said. "Even the donkeys are laughing at us."

"They mules, not donkeys," Antonio said.

The soldier shrugged. "Mule, donkey, same difference."

"Not really," Vadin chimed in. "A donkey is the offspring of two donkeys. But a mule is a cross between a horse and a donkey. They make the best pack animals."

"Well, I'll be damned," the soldier said. "Learn something new every day. But I still say they're laughing at this so-called rest area."

"So right," said another. "You won't see any of the higher-ups here. They're off to Naples for rest and recreation."

"Let's get a cup of tea, Antonio," Vadin offered. He had grown to like the homeless boy and the affectionate way he treated his mules.

"There is tea now?" Antonio said. It wasn't the usual mealtime.

Vadin smiled. "The cook's a friend of mine." He disappeared into the mess tent and came out with two steaming cups. They sat on a log by the creek and warmed their hands around the cups.

Antonio wanted to ask about the battle on Monte Cassino. How long would it go on? How long before the Germans were forced to retreat and he could go in search of Adriana? Certainly they'd shown no signs of giving in that he could see.

In his mind, he went over the English words to use. "You win battle soon, Vadin?" he said, finally.

Vadin considered, his brow furrowed. "You mean Monte Cassino? Not the way we're going at it. Those German paratroopers are tough – been through it all on the Russian front. They waited out the monastery bombing in their caves. I hear there wasn't one German casualty. Some of our own chaps were hit, though."

"Indian soldiers hit? But how . . . ?"

Vadin grimaced. "Typical foul-up. The bombers were supposed to come on the 16TH of February. At the last minute, they changed to the 15TH."

"I remember," Antonio said. "Day after Valentine's." He'd never forget that day.

"One of our companies was still dug in . . . not far from the monastery," Vadin recalled. "Twelve bombs fell on them; many were wounded. They told everyone but us that the planes were coming early.

"On top of that, we were ordered to attack right after the bombing. No time to bring up extra ammo and grenades. The higher-ups said it would take the Germans days to recover." Vadin's eyes flashed; it was the first time Antonio had seen him angry. "But they were just waiting. . . . It was a slaughter. And we were ordered back to attack again the next night — and the next. We lost more than seven hundred men and didn't gain a thing.

"The New Zealanders attacking the town were hammered too — by the guns on the mountain. A Maori company of two hundred tried to take the railroad station. Only seventy came back." He shook his head. "Bombing the monastery was a mistake. Now that the Germans are able to use the ruins, they're stronger than ever."

Antonio couldn't follow this stream of English. "Say more slow, please."

Vadin smiled. "Sorry, I forgot. I wish I could speak your language, but. . . ." He shrugged and tried again. "Jerries on Monte Cassino are too strong."

"Jerries?"

"Our name for Germans. Jerries are too strong. It's not possible to take Monte Cassino."

A wave of disappointment swept over Antonio. Would the German army always be there, between him and Adriana?

"But we'll still win," Vadin went on, "sooner or later. We've got more men and more firepower than they have."

Now Antonio was more confused than ever. *Win, not win, what did it all mean?*

Vadin saw his confused look. "What I mean is, we'll win, but not this way."

Antonio nodded. "Jerries on mountain too strong."

"That's right. We have to try something else."

"But how soon try something else?"

Vadin said he'd heard rumors of a huge offensive to bypass Monte Cassino. "Maybe April, maybe May," he said. "When the ground dries out, and the trucks and tanks can move again."

Antonio, like everyone else, would just have to wait and see.

The Sentry   19

Every day now, Domenic went to the fields in search
of dandelions. The *minestra* his mother made became
thinner and thinner. All she had left to cook with were the
dandelions and a few withered vegetables from the cellar.
Domenic's ribs looked like a washboard and his stomach
felt hollow. His sisters were listless, their faces pale.

His mother became increasingly desperate. "Somehow,
Domenic, we have to get one of the pots from the field,"
she said, finally.

"Yes, Mama." He tried to remember exactly where
the stone markers were that his father had put down when
they buried the pots in the fall.

"If the soldiers see us, they'll take the food for themselves," she said. "It will have to be at night."

"I'll do it," he said.

"I'll go with you. It'll be dangerous – there's always a sentry outside."

"No, it's better I go alone, Mama." He was taking his father's place, wasn't he? His father would have done it alone. "You must stay here with Angela and Pia. I can do it myself."

She looked doubtful. "Are you sure?"

"Of course," he said, with more bravado than he felt.

She sighed. "I suppose I should stay with the girls. Be very careful."

"I'll go tomorrow," he said. He tried not to think about stealing into the field in the dead of night. "First, I'll stay up late tonight and see what the sentry does."

He had to sit up – if he lay down, he knew he would fall asleep in an instant. Even so, his eyes closed on several occasions, and he jerked awake just in time to keep from toppling over. But by midnight, he had learned the sentry's routine: a circuit of the house every hour, the rest of the time by the front door, watching the road.

He would go the next night, as soon as the sentry finished his midnight round. That would give him almost an hour to get to the field, find a marker, dig up a pot, and come back.

The following night, he again had to force himself to stay awake. The time dragged slowly by, until it was midnight. Standing by the kitchen door, he watched the sentry pass on his midnight round. He waited five minutes, then gathered his nerve. As he grasped the doorknob, his mother's hand squeezed his shoulder, wordlessly encouraging him. He opened the door and slipped out.

Gently, Domenic pulled the door shut behind him. He waited, his hand on the knob, ready to retreat if he'd been heard. When nothing happened, he set out.

The night was black, the stars obscured by heavy clouds. The darkness closed in around him as he felt his way to the back of the house, where he'd put out the shovel earlier in the day. He picked it up and started across the garden.

The oak tree loomed in front of him like a many-armed giant. He could just make out the path beside it, a path worn smooth by a thousand trips to the fields. Treading quietly, he followed it, his eyes straining for the first stone marker, which his father had set close to the path.

He'd thought it would be easy to find, but, as the minutes passed, he worried that he'd missed it. He stopped and stood uncertainly, trying to orient himself.

It was hard to tell exactly where he was. Had he gone too far? Should he retrace his steps, or should he go on? Maybe someone had moved the marker. He could be out here for the whole hour searching, and return empty-handed to his disappointed mother. It began to rain.

Lost and bewildered by the darkness, he longed to flee to the safety of the house. In the distance, beyond the mountains, sheet lightning suddenly lit the sky. A moment later, the thunder arrived. It rumbled along the valley like the roll of a drum – a call to action.

Don't be such a coward, Domenic, he scolded himself, *you probably haven't gone far enough.* He walked resolutely on.

He hadn't gone far before he stumbled across the marker. Now all he had to do was turn left and go to the next one. He found that marker and began digging, mindful that he must go easy so as not to strike the pot hard and make a noise.

Another flash of sheet lightning, closer this time, lit the field. He froze. For an instant, he saw the outline of the house clearly. That meant the sentry at the house could see him too, if he happened to be looking this way.

The lightning faded and he resumed digging, but at every new flash he had to freeze. Finally he felt the shovel hit something. Kneeling down, he dug around the object with his hands until he could lift it out. It was a pot.

He set it on the ground and filled in the hole, roughening the earth so his digging wouldn't be obvious. Then he hoisted the heavy pot onto his shoulder, grabbed the shovel, and followed the path back to the house.

He was setting the shovel down behind the house when he heard footsteps. A shadowy figure emerged from around the corner and headed straight for him.

He caught his breath. Whoever it was would be on him in a moment. He wanted to bolt, but fear paralyzed his legs.

Abruptly, the figure halted. Neither Domenic nor the other moved. Then he heard the splash of a stream of urine. The soldier passed wind loudly, gave a satisfied sigh, and disappeared back around the corner.

Domenic waited long enough for him to return to the front, then crept to the kitchen door and slipped inside.

His mother was waiting anxiously. She took the pot and hid it under a pile of rags in a corner. "Thank the Lord you're back," she said. "Was it hard to find in the dark?"

He shrugged nonchalantly. "Not too hard."

⌘

The next morning, his mother waited until the soldiers left for their duties, then took the pot from its hiding place. She scooped out grain and potatoes and vegetables and cooked up a thick, nourishing *zuppa*. Domenic and his sisters hung over the bubbling pot, breathing in the aroma.

Serving it, Mama said, "Eat up, before the soldiers come back. For today, at least, we eat our fill. After today, I will have to ration it again."

Domenic felt full for the first time in months. His stomach had shrunk so much that he had to stop eating too soon. Still, it was a fine feeling to be satisfied. "But what about Papa and Guido?" he said. "Will they have anything left?"

His mother's eyes clouded. "I doubt it. They took some food with them, but it will be gone by now. Yet they dare not come back for more. I don't know what they can be eating."

"And the airmen are with them too, Mama."

"Yes, the airmen."

They sat silently. Domenic toyed with his empty bowl, thinking about his father and the others in the hut in the hills. "I could take some of ours to them, Mama," he said.

His mother looked up, surprised. Her son, she realized, was growing up. She must stop thinking of him as a little boy. "But you might get lost, or run into a German patrol."

"I'll be all right. I can find the way," he said. He sounded confident, but again doubts made his insides lurch. . . .

The Hideout

20

*D*omenic stopped. He was in the midst of a dense woods, which showed no sign of ending. Overhead, clouds blocked the morning sun, which had been visible earlier. When he'd started out, he thought he knew the way, but not being able to see the sun now didn't help. He'd kept it on his right before, which reassured him that he was heading north. He could be walking in circles, for all he knew.

He hitched the sack of food to the other shoulder. The German soldiers at the farm were used to seeing him with his sack for collecting dandelions, and he'd been able to walk away this morning without attracting attention. Had anyone stopped him to examine the sack, they would have been surprised to find, not dandelions, but potatoes and vegetables and flour, and a container of his mother's *zuppa*.

He kept going, hoping the woods would thin out soon. Ahead, something rustled in the undergrowth. *A small animal,* he thought, *a rabbit or a squirrel.* Then he saw the leg. He froze, afraid to move.

The leg was jutting out from behind a tree, its owner apparently sitting with his back against the trunk, invisible to Domenic except for the khaki-clad leg. *A soldier resting?* Domenic began to creep away, then he heard a moan and stopped.

Indecisive now, he waited, breathing heavily. Minutes passed. The leg shifted. Another moan, then an indistinct string of oaths. In Italian. The khaki pants, he saw, were bloodstained.

Emboldened, he edged closer. An arm came into view, a shoulder, then the back of a head. *Whoever he is, he needs help,* Domenic thought. He took a deep breath and stepped around the tree.

The man started, struggled to get to his feet, then gave up and sank back down. What he saw standing before him must have reassured him, for the startled look left his face.

They watched each other silently, then both spoke at once. *"Chi?"*

The man smiled. "You first." Domenic was relieved to hear the words in his own language.

"I'm Domenic," he said, placing his sack on the ground.

"And where do you live, Domenic?"

"On our farm."

The man shifted, wincing as he did so.

"What happened to your leg?" Domenic asked.

"Took a bullet. Give me a hand, will you?"

With Domenic's help, he struggled to his feet. But his face contorted with pain when he tried to put weight on his leg.

"What will you do now?" Domenic asked.

"Find somewhere I can rest this leg." He looked at Domenic speculatively. "Know any safe place near?"

Domenic hesitated. How much should he reveal? It seemed this man was a fugitive, and his khaki pants and tunic were those of a soldier. But how could he be sure which side he was on? "Our house is full of German soldiers," he said.

The man's face fell. "That's no good, then."

So he's not on the German side, Domenic thought. *Would it be safe to tell him about the hut?* He couldn't decide — it might endanger them all.

Picking up the sack, he started to edge away. "I have to go," he said, feeling badly about deserting the wounded man. "I . . . uh . . . I'm sorry, but I have to deliver something important." *If I can find the hut,* he thought.

The man seemed to read his thoughts. "That's okay," he said. "By the way, in case you're not sure where you are, there's a steep hill up ahead where the woods end." He pointed through the trees in the direction Domenic had been going. "I couldn't get up it with my leg, but you could. From the top, you might be able to see whatever it is you're looking for."

Now how did he know I was lost? Domenic wondered. As he turned to leave, he saw the man slump back down. Something about his forlorn expression made him turn and say, "Don't worry, I'll be back with help."

⌘

When he reached the top of the hill, Domenic surveyed the rugged countryside spread out before him. There, in a valley beyond, he could just make out the square shape of a small roof among the trees. He ran down the hill toward it, the sack bobbing up and down on his shoulder.

The hut sat silent. Was no one there? Or were they peering out to see who it was, poised to flee if necessary? He whistled, not wanting to approach without warning.

The door opened and his father stepped out and waved. "Is everything all right at home?" he asked anxiously, as Domenic hurried toward him.

"Yes, Papa." He was shocked at his father's thin and drawn appearance, but he supposed he himself looked even scrawnier. "I brought food for you." He slid the sack from his shoulder.

His father's lined face brightened. "Bless you. We need it badly."

His brother, Guido, and the airmen, Harry and Jerome,

came out to greet him. They exclaimed over the food, sniffing the container of thick soup in anticipation.

"Bring it inside," his father said.

"But there's something else first, Papa. A wounded man in the woods back there – a soldier. He needs help."

His father stopped at the door. "A soldier? German?"

"I don't think so. He speaks Italian."

"But who is he?"

Domenic shrugged. "I . . . I don't know. He's wearing army clothes . . . and he's been shot in the leg."

"What color army clothes?" Jerome asked.

"Khaki."

"Sounds like one of ours." Domenic suddenly realized that Jerome was speaking to him in Italian. Living with his father and Guido, the airman's grasp of the language was coming along.

His father didn't hesitate. "Let's go, then. You lead the way, Domenic."

"We'll come with you," Jerome said. "May have to carry him back."

As they were skirting the hill, Domenic's father asked if more German soldiers had arrived in their valley. Domenic told him then about the captain moving in with his unit and taking over the house.

His father looked shocked. "German soldiers living in our house! Your poor mother! And Angela and Pia! Are they all right?"

"Yes, Papa. The captain treats us politely." He decided not to tell about the corporal and the grenade just now.

⌘

The soldier was still slumped against the tree. He broke into a smile as they approached. "You're back, Domenic!" He held out his hand to the men. "Sergeant Marco Robinson. You have a good boy here."

Domenic's father stared at the hand for a moment before realizing he was meant to shake it. "Your leg is bleeding, Sergeant."

"The German doctor told me not to walk on it for a month, so they weren't guarding me too closely. It was easy to escape, but I'm paying for it now."

"We'll carry you to the hut," Domenic's father said. They gathered around to lift him, but the sergeant shook his head. "Just give me a hand up. Got this far on my own; I can make it the rest of the way."

In the hut, Jerome, who'd been trained in first aid, unwrapped the blood-soaked bandage. "Looks like the bullet went through the fleshy part of your thigh. Lucky it missed the bone."

While Jerome washed the wound as best he could, the sergeant was kept busy answering questions.

"I'm with the 1st Canadian Infantry Division," he said.

"Canadian!" Domenic's father looked up in surprise. "You speak Italian well."

"My mother's from Italy," the sergeant said. "She spoke Italian to us back home in Toronto. . . . Our division landed in Sicily almost a year ago. Took Sicily, then crossed to the mainland. The Germans tried to drive us back into the Mediterranean, but we hung on. Been fighting our way up Italy ever since, battle after battle. We just finished taking Ortona, on the Adriatic." He jerked his thumb toward the east. "That was the toughest fight yet." He sighed. "I'm tired of war – watching friends die."

"I know what you mean," Jerome said. He finished rewrapping the sergeant's wound. "Best I can do. Needs a fresh bandage and time to heal. How did it happen?"

The sergeant's brow furrowed. "The Germans were holed up in this village and the CO sent my platoon to clear them out. Had to cross an open field to get at them. No cover, no tank support. . . . But you don't want to hear all this."

Yes, we do, Domenic wanted to say. *Don't stop now.* He was too shy to speak up, but the airman Harry wasn't. "Then what happened?" Harry said.

The sergeant lay back and stared at the ceiling. "I told the Bren gunners to give us covering fire and we took off. All I remember is running, bullets tearing up the ground beside me. Worst were the rockets from their Nebelwerfers – Moanin' Minnies, we call them. They make a great bloody moaning noise like a bunch of ghosts coming at you. Anyway, I got there somehow, along with about half my platoon.

"Behind me, the rest were lying all over the field. One was screaming his head off for a medic. Made me mad as hell, what they'd done to my men. I ran to the first house, kicked open the door, and threw in a grenade. The door blew back in my face.

"When I came to, everything had quieted down. The other men had cleared out the rest of the village. Then I heard someone calling from inside the house. I thought it was a trap at first, but there was something in the voice. I went in."

The sergeant's eyes took on a faraway look. "Poor kid. He was sitting against the wall, his stomach split wide open. He had both his hands across it, like he thought he could hold the whole mess in, but most of his guts had spilled out on the floor."

Domenic winced. *So that's what war was really like.* Not all shiny leather boots and peaked caps and motorcycles and smart uniforms hung with medals.

"He was just a kid," Sergeant Marco went on. "Sixteen or seventeen. He looked up at me. I still remember his words . . . and I don't even understand German. '*Helfen Sie mir,*' he said. Found out later it means 'Help me.'

"I unhooked my canteen and held it to his mouth. He gulped down the water . . . mostly it ran out on the floor, along with more guts. 'Medics coming soon,' I said, though I knew he'd be dead before they got there. Then I patted his head and left. There wasn't anything more I could do for him.

"After that I wasn't mad at anyone anymore – except whoever it was that got him and me into this mess in the first place."

It was a minute or two before he took up the story again. "Anyway, those Jerries don't give up easy. Before we could bring reinforcements, they counterattacked. That's when I got hit in the leg. We held them off until we ran out of ammo, then I passed the order to the others to retreat.

"My leg had gone numb and I didn't have even a grenade to throw at them, so I surrendered." He looked up guiltily. "Never thought I'd ever do that."

"You did the right thing, Sergeant," Jerome said. "Live to fight another day." And everyone, even Domenic, murmured agreement.

"A German doctor bandaged up my leg and they sent me off to prison camp with the others. I felt lucky; some were barely alive – one poor soldier had lost both legs from a grenade, another was blinded by shrapnel and babbling. I pretended I couldn't walk. Then, when I saw my chance, I took off into the woods."

The sergeant shrugged. "That's about it. Been wandering for days. I figured I could find my way south by watching the sun, but the sun hardly ever came out. I was just about at the end of my rope when you found me."

Domenic's father stirred the thick soup. The sergeant sniffed the air. "Ah, that smells good – just like our kitchen back home when my mother's making *zuppa*."

"How long before the Allied army reaches us here, Sergeant?" Domenic's father asked.

The sergeant shrugged. "Monte Cassino's holding everything up. First the Yanks tried to take it. Then the East Indians on the mountain, and the New Zealanders in the town below. None of them got there, but it wasn't from lack of trying. A lot of brave men died."

"But if they can't take Monte Cassino, what can they do?" Harry wondered aloud.

The sergeant didn't hesitate. "Go around it somehow," he said. "When you're facing a crack paratroop battalion entrenched on a mountain, you'd better find some way around it."

"But with all those mountains on both sides of the valley . . . ?"

"The French have mountain troops that wanted to try," the sergeant said. "But I heard the big boss in charge of everything, General Alexander, vetoed that . . . said it couldn't be done."

Harry sighed. "Sounds like it's going to be a long wait, Sergeant. I keep telling Jerome here that we should take our chances on finding our own way back."

"Give it a little longer," the sergeant said. "I heard a rumor that something big was in the works. Don't know what, but let's hope it's different from what we're doing now."

Then Domenic bid good-bye and left for home. On the way, he thought about what Sergeant Marco had said. He hoped the "something big" would start soon.

Moving Up

21

*R*est was over for the Indian regiment. "We're heading out tomorrow," Vadin said.

"Monte Cassino again?" Antonio asked, expecting the worst.

"Not this time, thanks to the gods. Someone else's turn. The Free Polish are taking on Monte Cassino now. For us, it's the Liri Valley."

"And the mules? You need?"

"Sure do. To carry our equipment – as far as the Rapido River anyway."

The mule train set out at daybreak. Although the muddy roads had dried in the spring sunshine, now the train was plagued by choking dust. All day, a steady stream of troop trucks, gun carriers, and tanks clanked past, stirring up clouds of dust as they overtook the slow-moving mule train. Antonio tied a kerchief over his mouth and nose, and tried to do the same for his mules; they would have none of it.

They covered most of the distance that day. "You're to stay here for now," Vadin said to Antonio, when they stopped in a field. "The regiment's forming up by the river. We get our orders there. All I know is, I've been told to be in full battle gear." He went off to join his platoon.

Vadin came back just as the sun was setting. He looked tense. "I'll guide you to the river tomorrow," he said. "Then you wait there while we cross and move into the Liri Valley. That's the plan – if it works."

He didn't sound like it was going to be easy, Antonio thought.

"And one other thing. Tether the mules well tonight. There'll be a lot of noise later."

With his mules tethered, Antonio lay on the ground beside Mussolini. He found it hard to sleep, expecting "a lot of noise" at any time. The night dragged. He thought it must be well past midnight – he found out later it was exactly 11:00 P.M. on May 11TH – when, suddenly, the ground shook beneath him, the skies lit up, and a deafening roar enveloped him.

He leapt up. The flashes from the simultaneous firing of a thousand Allied guns blinded him; waves of sound assaulted his ears. The noise seemed to penetrate to the bone.

Tongues of flame leapt from long lines of camou-
flaged gun barrels to the rear, as from some fearsome array
of fire-breathing dragons. The countryside for miles
around was lit, as if an unseen hand had flicked on a celes-
tial switch. The *shush-shush-shush* of shells overhead was
unrelenting.

The terrified mules strained at their tethers, their eyes
wild. "Easy, easy," Antonio said to them, over and over.

The opening barrage went on for an hour. It was followed by intermittent firing for the rest of the night, as
the guns zeroed in on particular targets.

Sleepless, Antonio waited for dawn, wondering how
anyone on the receiving end of such a barrage could possibly survive. It could mean a quick victory over a crushed
enemy; it could make the battle less bloody for Vadin and
his companions, yet he couldn't shake the feeling that
such a murderous barrage, from any source, was the hand
of the devil himself.

Dazed by the night-long uproar, Antonio eventually
saw a different kind of light creep up the eastern sky. The
thunder of the guns continued, but the flashes faded in
the morning light, put in their place by the far greater
power of the rising sun.

The mule train slowly formed up, and the line of
mules and muleteers set off for the river, guided by Vadin.

⌘

They stayed between the two lines of white tape marking the path that had been cleared of mines. The landscape on either side was barren, churned up by shell fire, olive groves hundreds of years old reduced to shattered stumps. They hurried past a dead mule, thick with flies, its smell putrid.

As they pushed forward, the sounds of battle came closer. The morning ground mist lifted and the German artillery began to retaliate in earnest. The thundering bursts of shells from up ahead reminded Antonio of his nightmarish treks up Monte Cassino. With the arrival of daylight, the German spotters on the mountain could now see their targets below clearly.

As they approached the river, the scene was chaotic. Tanks and soldiers milled around, waiting for a bridge to be launched. A team of engineers worked frantically, bolting sections of the temporary Bailey bridge together on the bank, ignoring the shells dropping around them.

The advance was behind schedule. German resistance, heavier than expected, had caught the Allied army at daylight, without the necessary bridges in place.

A rubber boat loaded with soldiers paddled furiously across the fast-flowing water. As it closed on the far bank, Antonio heard the hoarse rasping of a German machine gun. The boat tilted and sank, and the soldiers were pitched into the water.

Loaded down with equipment, some never surfaced; others were swept downstream. A few made it to shore

and flung themselves onto the far bank, pinned there by
the German machine guns.

On the near bank, a shell landed beside the bridge
under construction with a shuddering crash, spraying
shrapnel. When the dust cleared, two of the engineers lay
on the ground.

"Stretcher bearer!" someone called. "Over here!"

Antonio stared at the prone bodies. Blood was pud-
dling around them.

Two medics ran up and dropped to their knees.
Checking the pulse of the first engineer, the medic shook
his head. *So sudden,* Antonio thought. One minute, the
engineer had been skillfully fitting a steel crosspiece into
place, the next he was dead.

The second engineer stirred and moaned as they lifted
him onto a stretcher. Others took their places, and the
work on the bridge continued until it was completed.

Guided by the gestures and shouts of the engineer in
charge, the bridge was pushed into place by a half-track –
a special truck with wheels on the front and tanklike
tracks on the rear. The bridge dropped off its rollers onto
the baseplates on either bank, and an engineer raced
across to bed it down.

Vadin's voice cut through the din. "Muleteers, you're to
wait here until we send for you." Then he formed up with
his platoon and they quick-marched across the bridge.
Antonio held his breath as a shell dropped into the river,

just missing the bridge and sending up a geyser of water.

The troops spread out on the far bank, crouching and firing at unseen targets. The _chug-chug_ of Brens and the screech of submachine guns mixed with the juddering crash of mortar bombs.

Two tanks appeared and clanked across the bridge, engines growling. "Canadian tanks," Antonio heard a soldier say. Reaching the far bank, the tanks forged straight ahead, the _blam-blam-blam_ of their guns gradually growing more distant. The Indian troops spread out and followed behind the tanks. Antonio watched Vadin until he was out of sight.

⌘

The battle gradually moved away from the river and the muleteers settled down to wait. Not until the next day did a guide come back to lead the mule train across the bridge and into the valley. It wasn't Vadin who came, however.

Antonio worried that something had happened to him. He asked the guide, who merely shrugged. "So many casualties . . . can't keep track."

Across the bridge, the broad plain of the Liri Valley spread out before them, but they were careful to keep within the two lines of white tape. The land was pock-marked with shell craters. They passed a burnt-out tank and, beyond it, an abandoned concrete pillbox. Beside the pillbox lay mangled bodies, sprawled in odd ways that left no doubt that this was death – a neck at an acute angle, arms outstretched, a gray-green face, a mouth open as if in surprise, an absolute stillness.

The smell of death was everywhere. Antonio turned away at the sight of a helmet with part of a head inside. He watched a Spitfire streak down, guns blazing at some target in the distance.

When they caught up with the rear guard of the Indian regiment, the equipment was unloaded. "Really need those," a soldier said, patting the boxes of ammunition on Mussolini's back. "Our men haven't stopped firing since yesterday morning. Neither have the Germans, unfortunately."

He spoke casually, as if they were on a training exercise, but Antonio noticed the way his hands shook as he fumbled at the ropes. The unloading was completed and the equipment sent forward. Again the mule train waited to see when they would be needed.

Night fell. The front line, a kilometer or so ahead, was constantly lit by exploding shells, mortar bombs, and tracers. The muleteers stretched out on the ground by their mules to sleep, trying to ignore the deadly conflict over the hill.

Antonio, however, wanted to see what was happening, what his friend Vadin was going through. He started up the hill behind which the mule train had settled.

"Keep your head down, if you're going up there," one of the rear guard warned.

Antonio lay in the grass at the top and tried to make sense of the frenzied activity ahead. Tracer bullets stitched the darkness, shell bursts lit the sky, and the chatter of machine guns was constant. *Was Vadin in the middle of that?* he wondered. *Was he even still alive?*

Suddenly, he heard a voice nearby. *"Nein, nein,"* it said in German. Almost a whisper, the voice was coming from somewhere off to his left. At first he could make out nothing in the dark, then he saw the outline of their helmets silhouetted against the sky as they slowly raised their heads above the grass. He counted three, maybe four of them, rifles poised.

"Nein, nein," the voice said again, and the rifles were lowered.

He hardly dared move, yet he had to warn the others. Would there be time? Very carefully, in slow motion, he pushed himself backwards down the hill, stopped, listened. Nothing but the blood pounding in his ears; no sign they'd heard him. He slid a little further, stopped, listened, slid again. In this way, he at last reached the bottom.

He crawled to the closest soldier, who seemed to be dozing sitting up. Antonio touched his shoulder gently. His eyes sprang open. "Wha —"

"Sh," Antonio whispered, then pointed back up the hill. "Jerries."

"Oh, hell. How many?"

Antonio held up three fingers, shrugged, added a fourth.

The soldier picked up his gun and silently woke a companion. The two of them, crouching low, set out to skirt the hill. Antonio soon lost their shapes in the dark.

They have the advantage, he thought. *They aren't silhouetted against the sky like the ones at the top of the hill. But will they get there before the Germans open fire? Oh, hurry, hurry.*

The minutes passed. Then, suddenly, the crack of rifles from the top of the hill. Antonio went rigid, expecting to feel the *thwack* of a bullet hitting his flesh.

The camp exploded into life. Soldiers leapt up, mules bucked and whinnied, muleteers ran here and there in confusion.

More firing, then shadows moving down the hill. "For God's sake, don't shoot; it's us," one of the shadows called out.

They brought two prisoners, eyes downcast, arms raised.

"Two more of them up there," one of the soldiers said, jerking his thumb back toward the hill. "Dead. A patrol doing a recce, I guess."

"If they'd opened fire, it would have been curtains for us," the other said. "It was this lad who warned us." He put a hand on Antonio's shoulder.

Antonio was just thankful they hadn't all been gunned down. But he couldn't get his mind off the two bodies on top of the hill. He remembered the *nein, nein* he'd heard and he felt a stab of guilt. Maybe the German patrol was only looking for information on the enemy positions . . . maybe they had no intention of shooting and giving away their presence.

He shook himself. *It's war, isn't it? It's kill or be killed, they say. You can't afford to feel guilty.* He went to Mussolini to calm her.

⌘

The next day, the mule train was still waiting for orders. For three days now, the Indian regiment had been fighting its way, little by little, up the Liri Valley. *How much longer,* Antonio wondered, *can they keep at it night and day?*

That morning, a line of fresh troops went by, heading for the front. They tramped past, single file, an orderly spacing between each man.

"Hey, the Canucks have finally arrived," an Indian soldier called out, good-naturedly. "Where you fellows been?"

"What are you doin' way back here, you guys?" one of the Canadians responded. "The front's up ahead."

"Next stop Rome, for us," another called out. "Can't wait for you."

"Quiet down back there," a Canadian sergeant called out. "It's silence once we get past this hill."

Antonio listened to their chatter. Going into battle yet joking about it seemed strange to him.

The first line of Canadian troops was followed, not long after, by more. Then, in the afternoon, the Indian troops the Canadians were relieving began returning.

Disheveled and weary, they straggled in. Antonio saw vacant stares, and, in some, a wild look. They flopped down behind the hill, not bothering to take off their packs.

Antonio searched the faces in vain for Vadin.

Another platoon arrived – some bandaged, some limping. Still no sign of Vadin. The remnants of a third platoon approached, walking as if it took a supreme effort to put one foot in front of the other.

Then he saw him. "Vadin!" Antonio raised his hand in greeting.

The briefest of smiles cracked Vadin's dirt-encrusted face. "Hello, Antonio," he said, then he flopped onto the ground and fell into a deep asleep.

A Strategic Retreat

22

*D*omenic, fast asleep in the kitchen of the farmhouse, was woken by a thunderous noise. At first, he thought it was a mammoth thunderclap, but the sound went on far too long to be thunder. He got up and felt his way around the sleeping forms of his sisters.

At the window, he blinked in disbelief. Frenzied flashes of light danced across the horizon to the south, as if a swarm of giant fireflies had gone berserk. Though he had no way of knowing it, he was witnessing the simultaneous firing of some sixteen hundred guns, opening the May 11TH Allied spring offensive. The roar of the barrage carried across the mountains and reverberated through the valley.

His mother, joining him at the window, gasped. "I pray to God they don't aim their guns here," she said.

Upstairs, where the captain and his staff slept, there was a sudden burst of activity. The radio crackled into life, and agitated voices carried down the stairs. The sergeant raced down and barked out orders to the sleeping soldiers spread around the ground floor. They sprang up. Outside in the lane, trucks and motorcycles roared to life.

Something big is happening, Domenic thought. *Could this be what Sergeant Marco had talked about, what they had been waiting for all winter?* He saw the captain jump in the staff car and drive away. It was dawn before he came back and took the stairs, two at a time, unrolling a map as he went.

Not long after, the lieutenant and the sergeant came down and hurried outside. Domenic, burning with curiosity, watched from the window as the sergeant shouted orders.

A squad of soldiers ran to the fields behind the house, where the antiaircraft guns and the bunkers had been installed. Some began taking down the camouflage nets over the guns; others disappeared into the bunkers and came out with machine guns and mortars. These were piled by the lane.

Domenic's heart leapt when he saw this, but he didn't say anything to his mother. *Soon enough,* he thought, *if they load everything on the trucks and drive away.*

Later that day he was glad he hadn't said anything, for the soldiers were still there. The big guns had been hauled as far as the lane, but the men were now standing around, smoking and talking. At supper time, they came back into the house and began their usual routine of heating meals in the fireplace. Nothing had changed.

That night, Domenic saw the captain pacing the house. He looked into the kitchen as if he was going to say something, then the radio crackled and he hurried back upstairs.

The next morning, as Domenic was bringing in water, the captain strode into the kitchen. "I have come to bid you good-bye," he said, formally. "May all go well with you, young man." And, turning to Domenic's mother, "And with you, Signora, and your daughters." Then he gave a slight bow and turned to go.

Mama stared in surprise. She seemed, for once, lost for words. Domenic's curiosity overcame his shyness. "Please, Captain, can you tell us what is happening?"

The captain turned back. He smiled wryly. "You might call it a tactical withdrawal. A strategic retreat to a new line of defense, so to speak."

Domenic didn't know what the military language meant, but he understood that they really were leaving. "And will you soon be able to watch your son play soccer, Captain?" he asked.

"No, not yet," the captain said. "But someday, I hope." Then he departed.

⌘

For the second time, Domenic approached the hut in the hills. It had been easier to find now that he knew the way and there were no German patrols to worry about.

"Papa!" he called.

His father opened the door a crack, looked around, then stepped out. "Is anything the matter, Domenic?" he asked, anxiously. "You're back so soon."

Domenic couldn't help smiling. "No, nothing is the matter, Papa. I came to tell you they've gone. The Germans have gone!"

At that, the door of the hut burst open and the two airmen rushed out with Sergeant Marco and Domenic's brother, Guido, on their heels.

"Gone? They've really gone?" They grouped around Domenic, waiting to hear more.

"Yes, they packed everything up," Domenic said, suddenly shy with all these men hanging on his every word. "They even took the guns from the fields. They left this morning. They went west. I watched until they were out of sight."

The group around him broke into cheers. They slapped each other on the back and shook hands, and Harry did a little dance.

Domenic's father was still cautious. "And have the Allied soldiers come?"

Domenic shook his head. "No one has come. We are alone."

His father frowned. "Then why did the Germans leave? Perhaps they will be back."

Sergeant Marco shook his head. "Not likely. I figure our boys have launched the big offensive – it probably started when we heard all those guns two nights ago. They may have broken through into the Liri Valley by now, or maybe the French mountain troops came out behind the German lines. Either would force the Germans to pull back, before they are cut off."

"Then you think it's safe for us to go home?" Papa asked hopefully.

"If there are no more Germans in the valley."

They all looked to Domenic for reassurance. He hesitated.

"Well, are there?" his father pressed.

"I . . . I don't know," he said. "I just know the ones that were at our house have gone."

"Maybe we should wait until we're sure," his father said.

Sergeant Marco nodded. "Yeah, we don't want to be taken prisoner by the last bunch of retreating Germans. They won't be in a good mood."

Everyone looked deflated. "We could go as far as the old mill," Jerome suggested. "And we could wait there until Domenic is sure there are no more German soldiers."

So it was agreed they would move to the old mill that night. Sergeant Marco beamed at Domenic. "Thanks for bringing us the news," he said. He patted him on the back. "You're a good soldier." And, with the sergeant's praise ringing in his ears, Domenic left for home.

⌘

He was almost there when he was startled by a scream from the direction of the house. Domenic broke into a run. As he came over the hill, he saw a German soldier leading Dolce away. Close behind, his mother was shrieking at him. The soldier ignored her and dragged Dolce up the lane.

No, not Dolce, please not Dolce. Not now, when it's nearly over, Domenic pleaded to himself.

He saw the soldier lead Dolce to the road, where a group of his companions were waiting. He raced up, grabbed Dolce's halter, and wrenched it out of the soldier's hand.

The soldier swung around. *"Geh!"* he growled.

Domenic stayed where he was, one arm hooked around Dolce's neck. "No."

The soldier pointed his rifle. *"Geh!"*

Domenic peered down the barrel of the gun, into the tiny circle of darkness out of which the bullet would burst.

His mother reached his side and gently took the halter from his hand. He could only stand and watch as the soldier snatched it back.

Packs were strapped onto Dolce's back and she was led away to join two other waiting mules, tended by an old muleteer. The procession moved off.

As he passed the stricken boy, the old muleteer murmured, "She'll be all right. I'll take good care of her."

His eyes moist, Domenic turned away.

"I thought we were through with soldiers stealing from us," his mother lamented. "Poor Dolce."

Domenic stared down the road in the direction from which the soldiers had come. Stretching into the distance, the road was empty. "Maybe that was the last of them, Mama," he said. Then he returned to the house, his heart heavy.

Liberation 23

*A*ntonio gazed down into the valley tucked between the hills. He was relieved to see no sign of the German army. He'd had enough of war and shelling.

Beside him, Mussolini waited patiently. Ahead of him, the Indian rifle company spilled onto the valley floor.

"We don't know what we'll find when we get there," Vadin had said to him, when the company was ordered to swing north and pursue the far end of the retreating German line. "They're pulling back in some places, in others they're still resisting. Can you believe the Germans actually left Monte Cassino voluntarily? When they found out the French had crossed the mountains and were about to enter the Liri Valley behind them, they pulled out of the monastery quietly in the night."

"This good news, Vadin," Antonio had said.

"Yes, but too bad the generals didn't figure it out four months ago, after all we went through trying to drive the Jerries off that mountain." There was a bitterness in his voice. "All those killed and wounded. Not only our men. Americans, New Zealanders, British. The Polish, too . . . at the end, the Poles fought like tigers, lost over a thousand men, but the Germans still held them off. Then one morning they found the monastery empty. Just walked in."

Now Antonio was relieved to see Vadin turn and give a thumbs-up. That meant it was all clear ahead. The mule train moved forward, Mussolini limping, but keeping up bravely.

Antonio was worried about Mussolini. Her limp was getting worse. As they were leaving the Liri Valley, a piece of shrapnel from a shell burst had grazed her right front leg. Though he had disinfected and bandaged the wound, the leg wasn't healing as it should.

What she really needed, he knew, was a good long rest. Working all winter on the mountain had taken its toll, and now this. He'd spoken to Vadin about resting her, but how could they when they were constantly on the move?

They descended into a pleasant valley. Farms dotted the landscape, their olive groves and vineyards beginning to green with the warming weather. Still, there was something desolate about the place. No sign of people.

Then, as they passed, faces began to appear at windows. Tentatively, a few people emerged, standing by their doors, watching uncertainly.

The soldiers waved, and suddenly the people understood. They ran to the road to greet them. Thin and haggard, their clothes in tatters, many barefoot, they laughed and cried, and embraced their liberators.

At one farm, a family waited at the end of their lane as the column of soldiers approached. The boy stopped Vadin and talked excitedly to him, pointing across the fields. Vadin couldn't follow his rapid stream of Italian. He called to Antonio. "Come and tell me what he's saying."

Antonio smiled at the boy to put him at ease. "What is it, my friend?"

The boy looked relieved to hear someone speaking his own language. He told his story, the words tumbling over each other in his hurry to get them out.

Antonio listened with growing interest. "Two British airmen and a Canadian sergeant," he repeated. "Under the very noses of the Germans! Good for you. What's your name?"

"Domenic," came the reply.

Antonio turned to Vadin and explained in English as best he could. "Domenic say they hiding British and Canadian from Germans. In old mill. Canadian wounded."

"A very brave thing to do," Vadin said. "Tell him to fetch them. We'll wait here."

Domenic dashed off, giving little leaps of exhilaration as he crossed the field.

"They'll be in no shape to walk all the way back to their units, especially the wounded one," Vadin said. "I'll see if I can arrange some transport."

By the time Vadin came back, Domenic was leading a small group of shabbily dressed men across the field. They were hurrying, almost running – except one, who trailed behind, limping.

Angela and Pia ran to their father and jumped into his arms. The whole family embraced. "It's over at last," Domenic's mother said. "And we're all still alive, thanks to the good Lord."

"And to the captain," said Domenic, though no one heard him.

Jerome and Harry, all smiles, shook hands with Vadin and Antonio. Sergeant Marco limped up, last of all. "Hey, you don't know how great it is to see you guys," he said, embracing Vadin and Antonio and anyone else who came near.

"These good people risked their lives for us," Jerome said, indicating the Luppino family. "They deserve a medal."

"I'll second that," Harry added. "They shared the little food they had, right to the end."

At the mention of food, Vadin unslung his pack and pulled out some packages. "Just army rations," he said, passing them out. "They may help." Domenic and his sisters got squares of chocolate. Their faces took on a rapturous look as the chocolate melted in their mouths.

A jeep pulled up beside them and a medic got out. He looked askance at the bloody rag around Marco's leg. "We'd better change that before it gets infected, Sergeant."

"It'll be okay," Marco said. "I just want a lift back to my unit."

"We have a first-aid post," the medic said. "Let me fix that wound up there, then we'll see about transport to your unit. Hop in. You too," he said to Jerome and Harry.

The airmen turned to the Luppino family. "How can we ever thank you enough . . . ," Jerome began. He hesitated, looking at Sergeant Marco. "You speak Italian much better than we do. Will you tell them, Marco, how much we appreciate what they did for us?"

"And tell them we'll stay in touch," Harry added, "after we get back to England."

Marco translated that and added more words of thanks of his own. Then, with much embracing and back-patting, he and the airmen climbed into the jeep and the medic drove away.

Antonio, meanwhile, was rummaging in the sacks on Mussolini's back. He came up with a bag of flour, sugar cubes, and a loaf of bread. "All right to give them this?" he said to Vadin, who nodded his approval.

He handed the food to Domenic's mother, who stared at the sugar, tears in her eyes.

Domenic, Antonio noticed, was stroking Mussolini's muzzle. "I see you're fond of mules," he said.

Domenic nodded. "She looks like our Dolce – same white muzzle, and just as friendly." He sighed, remembering. "The last German soldiers took Dolce with them . . . at gunpoint."

Vadin, meanwhile, was trying to communicate with Signore Luppino. He held up an empty container. "Water?" he asked. "Is the well working?"

Signore Luppino nodded vigorously. "Well working good. Domenic show you."

Domenic went with them to the well and primed it for them. Antonio watched him as he worked the pump. "Have any refugees from Monte Cassino passed this way, Domenic?" he asked. "I'm looking for a . . . a special friend . . . a girl . . . my age. We lost each other, after the monastery bombing. She was traveling with her grandmother, and some others from the monastery."

Domenic stopped and stared at his questioner. Antonio, obviously older than him, looked about the same age as Adriana. He was from Cassino, and was now working as a muleteer. A sudden jealousy seized him as he realized who he was talking to. *This must be Adriana's boyfriend – the one she wondered if she would ever see again.*

He hesitated before answering. "There *were* some refugees from Monte Cassino," he said finally. "But that was months ago."

Antonio looked up, suddenly hopeful. "And was there a girl my age with them?"

Domenic resumed his pumping. Why should he tell this stranger?

Antonio was waiting expectantly.

"I don't remember," he said. "There was a group of them."

He saw Antonio's shoulders slump, the crushed look on his face, and he remembered Adriana's forlorn expression when she talked about her friend in danger on the mountain.

He let go of the pump handle and turned to face Antonio squarely. "Now that I think of it," he said, "there *was* a girl with them. Long dark hair, and . . . and very beautiful."

"She was here!" Antonio exclaimed. The questions burst out. "Was she all right? Do you remember which way they went?"

"It's coming back to me now," Domenic said. And before he could change his mind, he told Antonio the whole story about the refugees arriving, and the washing, and the shells, and which direction they went when they left, and even the name of the valley where they'd been told they would find Adriana's relatives.

But when he accidentally blurted out her name, not really meaning to, he stopped suddenly, embarrassed. It was obvious that he'd remembered her all along.

Antonio gave Domenic a strange look. Then he broke into a smile. "Thank you for remembering. You've been a great help. Maybe I can do something for you someday." He patted Domenic on the back.

Domenic sighed. Seemed he was getting lots of pats on the back lately, but not much else. He returned to pumping, until Vadin and Antonio had filled all their containers.

Mussolini, who'd found a patch of new green grass to munch on, gazed up at Domenic as she chewed contentedly. He stepped down from the well and went to the shed where Dolce had stayed. When he came back, he had the currying brush in his hand and he began brushing Mussolini's thick coat. She stood quietly, enjoying the attention.

Antonio, watching, said something to Vadin. Vadin turned and looked at the boy and the mule together. "Okay with me," he said.

When the Indian company assembled to resume their march, it was short one mule.

⌘

Difficult as it was for Antonio to leave Mussolini after all they'd been through together, he knew it was for the best. Here on the farm, living quietly, her leg would have a proper chance to heal. And it was a way of thanking Domenic.

"You'll have a better life here with Domenic and his family," he said, laying his head on her mane. "But I will miss you. Such a fine brave girl." He stroked her once more, then he turned quickly and walked away.

Domenic was thrilled. "She needs care, and a long rest," Antonio had told him. "She shouldn't be worked until that leg is healed. Are you sure your parents will want a mule with a wounded leg?"

"Oh, yes," Domenic had said, without hesitation, sure he was doing the right thing. In his mind he was already changing Mussolini's name to Dolchezza – Dolchezza for sweetness – almost the same as Dolce, but different.

Later, Papa and the two boys went to the field and dug up pots of meat and vegetables and grains. The family sat around the table enjoying their best meal in years.

As Domenic scraped the last bit of meat and gravy from his plate, he thought about what he would do, now that the German army had gone. When the school reopened, as it surely would soon, he would see his friends again, and when Dolchezza's leg was healed, he could ride her to the school, and. . . .

Papa and Guido got up and headed outside. "Come and help, Domenic," his father said. "We're bringing your mother's chest of drawers back in."

He jumped up. "I'm coming, Papa."

The house would soon be almost the same as before. But, when evening came on and the light had dimmed, Domenic would sometimes glimpse the shadowy figure of the corporal by the fireplace, staring at him.

The End

Afterword

*A*t Monte Cassino, three neatly cared-for cemeteries hold the bodies of the soldiers killed in the fighting:

The Commonwealth cemetery on the outskirts of the town, overlooked by the monastery, is the burial place of the British, Canadian, East Indian, Ghurka, and New Zealand soldiers. There are 4,266 graves – among them, 284 unidentified that lie beneath memorial stones engraved only with the words *A Soldier of the 1939–1945 War, Known unto God.*

The German cemetery, on the road up the Rapido Valley, is the resting place of some 20,000 German soldiers. Its entranceway is graced by a haunting sculpture of a grieving mother and father.

The Polish cemetery, on the mountain behind the

monastery, is the burial site of more than 1,100 soldiers of the Free Polish Brigade.

⌘

Further away, along Route 6 on the way to Rome, are the French and Italian cemeteries, where the soldiers of those two nations are buried.

And in the American cemetery at Anzio, on the west coast, the thousands of GI's who died on Monte Cassino, and in the Rapido River crossing, lie with their comrades that fell at the Anzio beachhead.

⌘

As for the generals:

General Alexander was promoted to field marshal and later became governor-general of Canada.

General Freyberg was appointed governor-general of New Zealand.

And in the United States, General Mark Clark was cleared of blame for the Rapido River disaster that cost 1,330 casualties in a brief Congressional investigation insisted on by angry veterans. He became head of a prestigious military college.

⌘

It's estimated that some 200 civilian refugees were killed in the bombing of the monastery.

The elderly monk, who refused to leave with the others after the bombing, was occasionally seen wandering around the ruins by the German soldiers. He died there not long after.

When the war was over, the monastery was rebuilt by the Italian government. The rebuilding took ten years and followed the original design. Art treasures sent to the Vatican for safekeeping were returned, as were those found in a salt mine in Germany.

Cassino is now a busy town just off the Rome to Naples *autostrada*. In a valley to the north, near the town of Gallinaro, the old mill where the two British airmen were hidden is still there, though the roof is crumbling.

⌘

Domenic Luppino is a fictional character invented by the author. Some of his experiences in this story – particularly his daily trips to the old mill with food for the airmen, and his encounter with the corporal – are loosely based on the real-life experiences of Sandy Cellucci. It was Sandy's recounting of his experiences as a boy on a farm in German-occupied Italy that first inspired this story.